A SH[...]

The first shot went home nicely, aimed as exactly as a scientist finds a spot with his instruments. Where the moon's rays splashed across the bare right forearm of Bull, he sent a bullet that slashed through the great muscles. The revolver dropped from the nerveless hand of the giant, but Bull never paused. On he came, empty-handed, but with the power of death, as the little man well knew, in the fingers of his extended left hand. He came with a snarl, a savage intake of breath, as he felt the hot slash of Pete's bullet. But Reeve, standing erect like some duelist of old, his left hand tucked into the hollow of his back, took the great gambling chance and refused to shoot to kill.

He placed his second shot more effectively, for this time he must stop that tremendous body advancing upon him. He found one critical spot. Between the knee and the thigh, halfway up on the inside of the left leg, he drove that second bullet with the precision of a surgeon. The leg crumpled under Bull and sent him pitching forward on his face. Reeve swung his gun wide and leaned to see how serious the damage was.

But that fraction of a second brought him into another peril. The giant heaved up on his sound right leg and his sound left arm, and flung himself forward, two limbs dangling uselessly. With a hideously contorted face, Bull swung his left arm in a wide circle for a grip and scooped in Pete Reeve, as the latter sprang back with a cry of horror....

BULL HUNTER

LEISURE BOOKS **NEW YORK CITY**

A LEISURE BOOK®

July 1996

Published by special agreement with Golden West Literary Agency.

Dorchester Publishing Co., Inc.
276 Fifth Avenue
New York, NY 10001

Printed in the United States of America.

BULL HUNTER

Chapter One

Bulk and Sinew

It was the big central taproot which baffled them.

They had hewed easily through the great side roots, large as branches, covered with soft brown bark; they had dug down and cut through the forest of tenderer small roots below; but when they had passed the main body of the stump and worked under it, they found that their hole around the trunk was not large enough in diameter to enable them to reach to the taproot and cut through it. They could only reach it feebly with the hatchet, fraying it, but there was no chance for a free swing to sever the tough wood. Instead of widening the hole at once, they kept laboring at the root, working the stump back and forth, as though they hoped to crystallize that stubborn taproot and snap it like a wire. Still it held and defied them. They laid hold of it together and tugged with a grunt; something tore beneath that effort, but the stump held, and upward progress ceased.

They stopped, too tired for profanity, and gazed down the mountainside after the manner of baffled men, who look far off from the thing that troubles them. They could tell by the trees that it was a high altitude. There were no cottonwoods, though the cottonwoods will follow a stream for more than a mile above sea level. Far below them a pale mist obscured the beautiful silver spruce which had reached their upward limit. Around the cabin marched a scattering of the balsam fir. They were nine thousand feet above the sea, at least. Still higher up the sallow forest of lodgepole pines began; and above these, beyond the timber line, rose the bald summit itself.

They were big men, framed for such a country, defying the roughness with a roughness of their own—these stalwart sons of old Bill Campbell. Both Harry and Joe Campbell were fully six feet tall, with mighty bones and sinews and work-toughened muscles to justify their stature. Behind them stood their home, a shack always sets us to grubbing up roots; and if we ain't diggin' up roots, we got to get out old 'Maggie' mare and try to plow. Plow in rocks like them! Nobody but 'Bull' can do it."

"I didn't know Bull could do nothing," said the girl with interest.

"Aw, he's a fool, right enough," said Harry, "but he just has a sort of a head for knowing where the rocks are under the ground, and somehow he seems to make old Maggie hoss know where they lie, too. Outside of that he sure ain't no good. Everybody knows that."

"Kind of too bad he ain't got no brains," said the girl. "All his strength is in his back, and none is in his head, my dad says. If he had some part of sense he'd be a powerful good hand."

"Sure would be," agreed Harry. "But he ain't no good now. Give him an ax maybe, and he hits one or two wallopin' licks with it and then stands and rests on the handle and starts to dreaming like a fool. Same way with everything. But, say, Joe, maybe he could start this stump out of the hole."

"But I seen you both try to get the stump up," said the girl in wonder.

"Get Bull mad and he can lift a pile," Joe assured her. "Go find him, Harry."

Harry obediently shouted: "Bull! Oh, Bull!"

There was no answer.

"Most like he's reading," observed Joe. "He

don't never hear nothing then. Go look for him, Harry."

Big Harry strode to the door of the hut.

"How come he understands books?" said the girl. "I couldn't never make nothing out of 'em."

"Me neither," agreed Joe in sympathy. "But maybe Bull don't understand. He just likes to read because he can sit still and do it. Never was a lazier gent than Bull."

Harry turned at the door of the shack. "Yep, reading," he announced with disgust. He cupped his hands over his mouth and bellowed through the doorway: "Hey!"

There was a startled grunt within, a deep, heavy voice and a thick articulation. Presently a huge man came into the doorway and leaned there, his figure filling it. There was nothing freakish about his build. He was simply over-normal in bulk, from the big head to the heavy feet. He was not more than a youth in age, but the great size and the bewildered puckering of his forehead made him seem older. The book was still in his hand.

"Hey," returned Harry, "we didn't call you out here to read to us. Leave the book behind!"

Bull looked down at the book in his hand, seemed to waken from a trance, then, with a muffled sound of apology, dropped the book behind him.

"Come here!"

French bread that the adventurer had eaten with the pseudo-merchant.

But to step out of that world of words into this keen sunlight—ah, there was the difference! The minds which one found in the pages of a book were understandable. But the minds of living men—how terrible they were! One could never tell what passed behind the bright eyes of other human beings. They mocked one. When they seemed sad they might be about to laugh. The minds of the two brothers eluded him, mocked him, slipped from beneath the slow grasp of his comprehension. They whipped him with their scorn. They dodged him with their wits. They bewildered him with their mockery.

But they were nothing compared with the laughter of the girl. It went through him like the flash and point of Le Balafré's long sword. He was helpless before that sound of mirth. He wanted to hold up his hands and cower away from her and from her dancing eyes. So he stood, ponderous, tortured, and the three pairs of clear eyes watched him and enjoyed his torture. Better, far better, that dark castle in ancient France, and the wicked Oliver and the yet more wicked Louis.

"Lay hold on that stump," shouted Harry.

He heard the directions through a haze. It was twice repeated before he bowed and set his great hands upon the ragged projections, where the side roots had been cut away. He settled his grip and waited. He was glad because this bowed position gave him a chance to look down to the ground and avoid their cruel eyes. How bright those eyes were, thought Bull, and how clearly they saw all things! He never doubted the justice behind their judgments of him; all that Bull asked from the world was a merciful silence—to let him grub in his books now and then, or else to tell him how to go about some simple work, such as digging with a pick. Here one's muscles worked, and there was no problem to disturb wits which were still gathering wool in the pages of some old tale.

But they were shrilling new directions at him; perhaps they had been calling to him several times.

"You blamed idiot, are you goin' to stand there all day? We didn't give you that stump to rest on. Pull it up!"

He started with a sense of guilt and tugged up. His fingers slipped off their separate grips, and the stump, though it groaned against the taproot under the strain, did not come out.

"It don't seem to budge, somehow," said Bull in his big, soft, plaintive voice. Then he waited for the laughter. There was always laughter, no matter what he did or said, but he never grew calloused against it. It was the one pain which ever pierced the mist of his brain and cut him to the quick. And he was right. There was laughter again. He stood suffering mutely under it.

The girl's face became grave. She murmured to Harry: "Ever try praisin' to big stupid?"

"Him? Are you joshin' me, Jessie? What's he ever done to be praised about?"

"You watch!" said the girl. Growing excited with her idea, she called: "Say, Bull!"

He lifted his head, but not his eyes. Those eyes studied the impatient feet of the girl's mustang; he waited for another stroke of wit that would bring forth a fresh shower of laughter at his expense.

"Bull, you're mighty big and strong. About the biggest and strongest man I ever see!"

Was this a new and subtle form of mockery? He waited dully.

"I seen Harry and Joe both try to pull up that root, and they couldn't so much as budge it. But I bet you could do it all alone, Bull! You just try! I bet you you could!"

It amazed him. He lifted his eyes at length; his face suffused with a flush; his big, cloudy eyes were glistening with moisture.

"D'you mean that?" he asked huskily.

For this terrible, clear-eyed creature, this mocking mind, this alert, cruel wit was actually speaking words of confidence. A great, dim joy welled up in the heart of Bull Hunter. He shook the forelock out of his eyes.

"You just try, will you, Bull?"

"I'll try!"

He bowed. Again his thick fingers sought for a grip, found places, worked down through the soft dirt and the pulpy bark to solid wood, and then he began to lift. It was a gradual process. His knees gave, sagging under the strain from the arms. Then the back began to grow rigid, and the legs in turn grew stiff, as every muscle fell into play. The shoulders pushed forward and down. The forearm, revealed by the short sleeve, showed a bewildering tangle of corded muscle, and, at the wrist, the tendons sprang out as distinct and white as the new strings of a violin.

The three spectators were undergoing a change. The suppressed grins of the two brothers faded. They glanced at the girl to see if she were not laughing at the results of her words to big Bull, but the girl was staring. She had set that mighty power to work, and she was amazed by the thing she saw. And they, looking back at Bull, were amazed in turn. They had seen him lift great logs, wrench boulders from the earth. But always it had been a proverb with the Campbell family that Bull would make only one attempt and, failing in the first effort, would try no more. They had never seen the mysterious resources of his strength called upon.

Now they watched first the settling and then the expansion of the body of their big cousin. His shoulders began to tremble; they heard deep, harsh panting like the breathing of a horse as it tugs a ponderous load up a hill, and still he had not reached the limit of his power. He seemed to grow into the soil, and his feet ground deeper into the soft dirt, and ever there was something in him remaining to be tapped. It seemed to the brothers to be merely vast, unexplored recesses of muscle, but even then it was a prodigious thing to watch the strain on the stump increase moment by moment. That something of the spirit was being called upon to aid in the work was quite beyond their comprehension.

There was something like a groan from Bull—a queer, animal sound that made all three spectators shiver where they stood. For it showed that the limit of that apparently inexhaustible strength had been reached and that now the anguish of last effort was going into the work. They saw the head bowed lower; the shoulders were now bunching and swelling up on either side.

Then came a faint rending sound, like cloth slowly torn. It was answered by something strangely like a snarl from the laborer. Something jerked through his body as though a whip had been flicked across his back. With a great rending and a loud snap the big stump came up. A little shower of dirt spouted up with the parting of the taproot. The trunk was flung high, but not out of the hands of Bull Hunter. He whirled it around his head, laughing. There was a ring and clearness in that laughter that they had never heard before. He dashed the stump on the ground.

"It's out!" exclaimed Bull. "Look there!"

He strode upon them. As he straightened up he became huger than ever. They shrank from him—from the veins which still bulged on his forehead and from the sweat and pallor of that vast effort. The very mustang winced from this mountain of a man who came with a long, sweeping, springing stride. On his face was a strange joy as of the explorer who tops the mountains and sees the beauty of the promised land beneath him. He held out his hand.

"Lady, I got to thank you. You—taught me how!"

But she shrank from his outstretched hand— as though she had labored to a larger end than she dreamed and was terrified by the thing she had made.

"You—you got a red stain on your hands. Oh!"

He came to a stop sharply. The sharp edges, where the roots had been cut away had worked through the skin and his hands were literally caked with mud and stained red. Bull looked down at his hands vaguely.

It came to Harry that Bull was taking up a trifle too much of Jessie's attention. The next thing they knew she would be inviting him to come to the next dance down her way, and they would have the big hulk of a man shaming himself and his uncle's family.

"Go on back to the house," he ordered sharply. "We don't have no more need of you."

Bull obeyed, stumbling along and still looking down at his wounded hands.

Chapter Two

Waking Up

He left the three behind him, bewildered and frightened. Had lightning split a thick tree beside them, or an unexpected landslide thundered past and swept the ground away at their feet, they could have been hardly more disturbed.

"Who'd of thought he could act like that!" remarked Joe. "My gosh, Jessie!"

They went and looked at the hole where the stump had stood. At the bottom was the white remnant of the taproot where it had burst under the strain.

"It wasn't so much how he pulled up the

stump," said the girl faintly. "But—but did you see his face, boys, after he heaved the stump up? I—just pick that stump up, will you?"

They went to the misshapen, ragged monster and lifted it, puffing under the weight.

"All right."

They dropped it obediently.

"And he—he just swung it around his head like it was nothing!" declared the girl. "Look how it smashed into the gravel where he threw it down! Why—why—I didn't know men was made like that. And his face—the way he laughed—why he didn't look like no fool at all, boys. But just as if he'd waked up!"

"You act so interested," said Harry Campbell dryly, "that maybe you'd like to have us call him out again so's you can talk to him?"

Apparently she did not hear, but stared down into the mist of the late afternoon, warning her that she must start home. She seemed puzzled and a little frightened. When she left them it was with a wave of the hand and with no word of farewell. They watched her go down the trail that jerked back and forth across the pitch of the slope; twice her pony stumbled, a sure sign that the rider was absentminded.

"Jessie didn't seem to know what to make of it," said Harry.

"Neither do I," returned his brother.

Both of them spoke in subdued voices as if

they were afraid of being overheard.

"And think if he'd ever lay a hold on one of us like that!" said Harry. He went to the stump and examined the side of one of the roots. It was stained with crimson.

"Look where his finger tips worked through the dirt and the bark, right down to the solid wood," murmured Joe.

They looked at each other uneasily. "My gosh," said Joe, "think of the way I handled him the other night! He—he let me trip him up and throw him!" He shuddered. "Why, if he'd laid hold of me just once, he'd of squashed my muscles like they was rotten fruit!"

Of one accord they turned back to the house. At the door they paused and peered in, as into the den of a bear. There sat Bull on the floor— he risked his weight on none of the crazy chairs—still looking at his stained hands. Then they drew back and again looked at each other with scared eyes and spoke in undertones.

"After this maybe he won't want to foller orders. Maybe he'll get sort of free and easy and independent."

"If he does, you watch dad give him his marching orders. Dad won't have no one lifting heads agin' him."

"Neither will I," snapped Joe. "I guess we own this house. I guess we support that big hulk. I'm going to try him right quick."

He went back to the door of the shack. "Bull, they ain't any wood for the stove to-night. Go chop some quick."

The floor squeaked and groaned under Bull's weight as he rose, and again the brothers looked to each other.

"All right," came cheerily from Bull Hunter.

He came through the door with his ax and went to the log pile. The brothers watched him throw aside the top logs and get at the heavier trunks underneath. He tore one of these out, laid it in place, and the sun flashed on the swift circle of the ax. Joe and Harry stepped back as though the light had blinded them.

"He didn't never work like that before," declared Joe.

The ax was buried almost to the haft in the tough wood, and the steel was wrenched out with a squeak of the metal against the resisting wood. Again the blinding circle and the indescribable sound of the ax's impact, slicing through the wood. A great chip snapped up high over the shoulder of the chopper and dropped solidly to the ground at the feet of the brothers. Again they exchanged glances and drew a little closer together. The log divided under the shower of eating blows, and Bull attacked the next section.

Presently he came to a pause, leaning on the handle of the ax and staring into the distance.

At this the brothers sighed with relief.

"I guess he ain't changed so much," said Harry. "But it was queer, eh? Kind of like a bear waking up after he'd been sleeping all winter!"

They jarred Bull out of his dream with a shout and set him to work again; then they started the preparations for the evening meal. The simple preparations were soon completed, but after the potatoes were boiled, they delayed frying the bacon, for their father, old Bill Campbell, had not yet returned from his hunting trip and he disliked long-cooked food. Things had to be freshly served to suit Bill, and his sons dared the wrath of Heaven rather than the biting reproaches of the old man.

It was strange that Bill delayed his coming so long. As a rule he was always back before the coming of evening. An old and practiced mountaineer, he had never been known to lose sense of direction or sense of distance, and he was an hour overdue when the sun went down and the soft, beautiful mountain twilight began.

There were other reasons which would ordinarily have disturbed Bill and brought him home even ahead of time. Snow had fallen heavily above timber line a few days before, and now the keen whistling of the wind and the swift curtaining of clouds, which was drawing across the sky, threatened a new storm that might even reach down to the shack.

And yet no Bill appeared.

The brothers waited in the shack, and the darkness was increasing. Any one of a number of things might have happened to their father, but they were not worried. For one thing, they wasted no love on the stern old man. They knew well enough that he had plenty of money, but he kept them here to a dog's life in the shack, and they hated him for it. Besides, they had a keen grievance which obscured any worry about Bill—they were hungry, wildly hungry. The darkness set in, and the feeble light wandered from the smoked chimney of the lantern and made the window black.

Outside, the wind began to scream, sighing in the distance among the firs, and then pouncing upon the cabin and shaking it as though in rage. The fire would smoke in the stove at every one of these blasts, and the flame leaped in the lantern.

Bull Hunter had to lean closer to the light and frown to make out the print of his book. The sight of his stolid immobility merely sharpened their hunger, for there was never any passion in this hulk of a man. When he relaxed over a book the world went out like a snuffed candle for him. He read slowly, lingering over every page, for now and again his eyes drifted away from the print, and he dreamed over what he had read. In reality he was not reading for the plot, but for the pictures he found, and he dreaded coming to the end of a book also, for books were rare in his life. A scrap of a magazine was a treasure. A full volume was a nameless delight.

And so he worked slowly through every paragraph and made it his and dreamed over it until he knew every thought and every picture by heart. Once slowly devoured in this way, it was useless to reread a book. It was far better to simply sit and let the slow memory of it trail through his mind link by link, just as he had first read it and with all the embroiderings which his own fancy had conjured up.

Often this stupid pondering over a book would madden the two brothers. It irritated them till they would move the lantern away from him. But he always followed the light with a sigh and uncomplainingly settled down again. Sometimes they even snatched the book out of his hands. In that case he sat looking down at his empty fingers, dreaming over his own thoughts as contentedly as though the living page were in his vision. There was small satisfaction in tormenting him in these ways.

Tonight they dared not bother him. The stained hands were still in their minds, and the tremendous, joyous laughter as he whirled the stump over his head still rang in their ears. But they watched him with a sullen envy of his immobility. Just as a man without an overcoat envies the woolly coat of a dog on a windy December day.

Only one sound roused the reader. It was a sudden loud snorting from the shed behind the house and a dull trampling that came to him through the noise of the rising wind. It brought Bull lurching to his feet, and the stove jingled as his weight struck the yielding center boards of the floor. Out into the blackness he strode. The wind shut around him at once and plastered his clothes against his body as if he had been drenched to the skin in water. Then he closed the door.

"What brung him to life?" asked Harry.

"Nothin'. He just heard ol' Maggie snort. Always bothers him when Maggie gets scared of something—the old fool!"

Maggie was an ancient, broken-down draft horse. Strange vicissitudes had brought her up into the mountains via the logging camp. She was kept, not because there was any real hauling to be done for Bill Campbell, but because, having got her for nothing, she reminded him of the bargain she had been. And Bull, apparently understanding the sluggish nature of the old mare by sympathy of kind, used to work her to the single plow among the rocks of their clearing. Here, every autumn, they planted seed that never grew to mature grain. But that was

Bill Campbell's idea of making a home.

Presently Bull came back and settled with a slump into his old place.

"Going to snow?" asked Harry.

"Yep."

"Feel it in the wind?"

It was an old joke among them, for Bull often declared with ridiculous solemnity that he could foretell snow by the change in the air.

"Yep," answered Bull, "I felt it in the wind."

He looked up at them, abashed, but they were too hungry to waste breath with laughter. They merely sneered at him as he settled back into his book. And, just as his head bowed, a far shouting swept down at them as the wind veered to a new point.

"Uncle Bill!" said Bull and rose again to open the door.

The others wedged in behind his bulk and stared into the blackness.

Chapter Three

A King Abdicates

They stood with the wind taking them with its teeth and pressing them heavily back. They could hear the fire flare and flutter in the stove; then the wind screamed again, and the wail came down to them.

"Uncle Bill!" repeated Bull and, lowering his head, strode into the storm.

The others exchanged frightened glances and then followed, but not outside of the shaft of light from the door. In the first place it was probably not their father. Who could imagine Bill shouting for help? Such a thing had never been dreamed of by his worst enemies, and they

31

knew that their father's were legion. Besides it was cold, and this was a wild-goose chase which meant a chilled hide and no gain.

But, presently, through the darkness they made out the form of a horseman and the great bulk of Bull coming back beside him. Then they ran out into the night.

They recognized the hatless, squat figure of their father at once, even in the dark, with the wind twitching his beard sideways. When they called to him he did not speak. Then they saw that Bull was leading the horse.

Plainly something was wrong, and presently they discovered that Bill Campbell was actually tied upon his horse. He gave no orders, and they cut the ropes in silence. Still he did not dismount.

"Bull," he commanded, "lift me off the hoss!"

The giant plucked him out of the saddle and placed him on the ground, but his legs buckled under him, and he fell forward on his face. Any of the three could have saved him, but the spectacle of the terrible old man's helplessness benumbed their senses and their muscles.

"Carry me in!" said Bill at last.

Bull lifted him and bore him gingerly through the door and placed him on the bunk. The light revealed a grisly spectacle. Crimson stains and dirt literally covered him; his left leg was bandaged below the knee; his right shoulder was roughly splinted with small twigs and swathed in cloth.

The long ride, with his legs tied in place, had apparently paralyzed his nerves below the hips. He remained crushed against the wall, his legs falling in the odd position in which they were put down by Bull. It was illustrative of his character that, even in this crisis, not one of the three dared venture an expression of sympathy, a question, a suggestion.

Crumpled against the wall, his head bowed forward and cramped, the stern old man still controlled them with the upward glance of his eyes through the shag of eyebrows.

"Gimme my pipe," he commanded.

Three hands reached for it—pipe, tobacco, matches were proffered to him. Before he accepted the articles he swept their faces with a glance of satisfaction. Without attempting to change the position, which must have been torturing him, he filled the pipe bowl, his fingers moving as if he had partially lost control of them. He filled it raggedly, shreds of tobacco hanging down around the bowl. He bent his head to meet the left hand which he raised with difficulty, then he tried to light a match. But he seemed incapable of moving the sulphur head fast enough to bring it to a light with friction. Match after match crumbled as he continued his efforts.

"Here, lemme light a match for you, dad!"

Harry's offer was received with a silent curling of the lips and a glint of the yellow teeth beneath that made him step back. The old man continued his work. There were a dozen wrecked matches before the blood began to stir in his numbed arm and he was able to light the match and the pipe. He drew several breaths of the smoke deep into his lungs. For the moment the savage, hungry satisfaction changed his face; they could tell by that alteration what agonies he had been suffering before.

Presently he frowned and set about changing his position with infinite labor. The left leg was helpless, and so was the right arm. Yet, after much labor, he managed to stuff a roll of the blankets into the corner and then shift himself until his back rested against this support. But his strength deserted him again. His pipe was dropped down in the left hand, his head sagged back.

Still they dared not approach him. His two sons stood about, shifting from one foot to another, as if they expected a blow to descend upon them at any moment; as if each labored movement of terrible old Bill Campbell caused them the agony which he must be suffering.

As for Bull Hunter, he sat again on the floor, his chin dropped upon his great fist, and wondered for a time at his uncle. It was the second great event to him, all in one day. First he had discovered that by fighting a thing, one can actually conquer. Second, he discovered that that great fighter, his uncle, had been beaten. The impossible had happened twice between one sunrise and sunset.

But men and the affairs of men could not hold his eye overlong. Presently he dropped his head again and was deep in the pages of his book. At length Bill Campbell heaved up his head. It was to glare into the scared faces of his sons.

"How long are you goin' to keep me waiting for my food?"

The order snapped them into action. They sprang here and there, and presently the thick slices of bacon were hissing on the pan, and the clouds of bacon smoke wafted through the cabin. When they reached Bill Campbell he blinked. Pain had given him a maddening appetite, yet he puffed steadily on his pipe and said nothing.

The tin plate of potatoes and bacon was shoved before him, and the big tin cup of coffee. The three younger men sat in silence and devoured their own meal; the two sons swiftly, but Bull Hunter fell into musings, and part of his food remained uneaten. Then his glance wandered to his uncle and saw a thing to wonder at—a horrible thing in its own way.

The nerveless left hand of the mountaineer, which had barely possessed steadiness to light a match, was far too inaccurate to handle a fork; and Bull saw his uncle stuffing his mouth with his fingers and daring the others to watch him.

Something like pity came to Bull. It was so rare an emotion to connect with human beings that he hardly recognized it, for men and women, as he knew them, were brilliant, clever creatures, perfectly at home in the midst of difficulties that appalled him. But, as he watched the old man feed himself like an animal, the emotion that rose in Bull was the sadness he felt when he watched old Maggie stumbling among the rocks. There was something wrong with the forelegs of Maggie, and she was only half a horse when it came to going downhill on broken ground. He had always thought of the great strength that once must have been hers, and he pitied her for the change. He found himself pitying Uncle Bill Campbell in much the same way.

When Bill raised his tin cup he spilled scalding coffee on his breast. The old man merely set his teeth and continued to glare his challenge at the three. But not one of the three dared speak a word, dared make an offer of assistance.

What baffled the slow mind of Bull Hunter

was the effort to imagine a force so great that battle with it had reduced the invincible Campbell to this shaken wreck of his old self. Mere bullets could tear wounds in flesh and break bones; but mere bullets could not wreck the nerves of a man so that his hand trembled as if he were drunk or hysterical with weariness.

He tried to work out this problem. He conceived a man of gigantic size, vast muscles, inexhaustible strength. The power of a bear and the swift cunning of a wild cat—such must have been the man who struck down Uncle Bill and sent him home a shattered remnant of his old self.

There was another mystery. Why did the destroyer not finish his task? Why did he take pity on Uncle Bill Campbell and bind up the wounds he had himself made? Here the mind of Bull Hunter paused. He could not pass the mysterious idea of another than himself pitying Uncle Bill. It was pitying a hawk in the sky.

Harry was taking away the dishes and throwing them in the little tub of lukewarm water where the grease would be carelessly soused off them.

"Did you get up that stump?" asked Uncle Bill suddenly.

There was a familiar ring in his voice. Woe to them if they had not carried out his orders! All three of the young men quaked, and Bull laid aside his book.

"We done it," answered Joe in a quavering voice.

"You done it?" asked Bill.

"We—we dug her pretty well clear, then Bull pulled her up."

Some of the wrath ebbed out of the face of Bill as he glanced at the huge form of Bull. "Stand up!" he ordered.

Bull arose.

The keen eye of the old man went over him from head to foot slowly. "Some day," he said slowly, speaking entirely to himself. "Some day—maybe!"

What he expected from Bull "some day" remained unknown. The dishwashing was swiftly finished. Then Uncle Bill made a feeble effort to get off his boots, but his strength had been ebbing for some time. His sons dared not interfere as the old man leaned slowly over and strove to tug the boot from his wounded leg; but Bull remembered, all in a flood of tenderness, some half dozen small, kind things that his uncle had said to him.

That was long, long ago, when the orphan came into the Campbell family. In those days his stupidity had been attributed largely to the speed with which he had grown, and he was expected to become normally bright later on;

and in those days Bill Campbell occasionally let fall some gentle word to the great boy with his big, frightened eyes. And the half dozen instances came back to Bull in this moment.

He stepped between his cousins and laid his hand on the foot of his uncle. It brought a snarl from the old man, a snarl that made Bull straighten and step back, but he came again and put aside the shaking hand of Uncle Bill. His cousins stood at one side, literally quaking. It was the first time that they had actually seen their father defied. They saw the huge hand of Bull settle around the leg of their father, well below the wound and then the grip closed to avoid the danger of opening the wound when the boot was worked off. After this he pulled the tight riding boot slowly from the swollen foot.

Uncle Bill was no longer silent. The moment the big hand of his nephew closed over his leg he launched a stream of curses that chilled the blood and drove his own sons farther back into the shadow of the corner. He demanded that they stand forth and tear Bull limb from limb. He disinherited them for cowardice. He threatened Bull with a vengeance compared with which the thunderbolt would be a feeble flare of light. He swore that he was entirely capable of taking care of himself; that he would step down into his grave sooner than he nursed and petted by any living human being.

All the while, the great Bull leaned impassively over the wounded man and finally worked the boot free. That was not all. Uncle Bill had slipped over until he could reach a billet of wood beside his bunk. He struck at Bull's head with it, but the stick was brushed out of his palsied fingers with a single gesture, and, while Uncle Bill groaned with fury and impotence, Bull continued the task of preparing him for bed. He straightened the old body of the terrible Campbell; he heated water in the tub and washed away stains and dirt; he took off the stained bandages and replaced them with clean ones.

His cousins helped in the latter part of this work. Weakness had reduced Uncle Bill to speechlessness. Finally the head of Bill Campbell was laid on a double fold of blanket in lieu of a pillow. A pipe had been tamped full and lighted by Bull and—crowning insult—set between Bill's teeth. When all this was accomplished Bull retired to his corner, picked up his book, and was instantly absorbed.

In the hushed atmosphere it seemed that a terrible blow had fallen, and that another was about to fall. Harry and Joe were as men stunned, but they looked upon their father with a gathering complacency. They had found it demonstrated that it was possible to disobey their father without being instantly destroyed.

They were taking the lesson to heart. And indeed old Bill Campbell himself seemed to be slowly admitting that he was beaten.

The illusion of absolute self-sufficiency, which he had built up through the years for the sake of imposing upon his sons and Bull Hunter, was now destroyed. At a single stroke he had been exposed as an old man, already beaten in battle by a foeman and now requiring as much care as a sick woman. The shame of it burned in him; but the comfort of the smoothed bunk and the filled pipe between his teeth was a blessing. He found to his own surprise that he was not hating Bull with a tithe of his usual vigor. He began to realize that he had come to the end of his period of command. When he left that sick bed he could only advise.

As a king about to die he looked at his heirs and found them strong and sufficient and pleasing to the eye. Nowhere in the mountains were there two boys as tall, as straight, as deadly with rifle and revolver, as fierce, as relentless, as these two boys of his. He had sharpened their tempers, and he rejoiced in the sullen ferocity with which they looked at him now, unloving, cunning, biding their time and finding that it had almost come. But he was not yet done. His body was wrecked; there remained his mind, and they would find it a great power. But he did not talk until the lights had been put out and the three youths were in their separate bunks. Then, without the light to show them his helpless body, in the darkness, which would give his mind a freer play, he began to tell his story.

It was a long narrative. Far back in the years he had prospected with a youth named Pete Reeve. They had located a claim and they had gone to town together to celebrate. In the celebration he had drunk with Reeve till the boy was stupefied. Then he had induced Reeve to gamble for his share of the claim and had won it. Afterward Pete swore to be even with him. But the years had gone by without another meeting of the men.

Only today, riding through the mountains, he had come on a dried-up wisp of a man with long, iron-gray hair, a sharp, withered face, and hands like the claws of a bird. He rode a fine bay gelding, and had stopped Bill to ask some questions about the region above the timber line because he was drifting south and intended to cross the summits. Bill had described the way, and suddenly, out of their talk, came the revelation of their identities—the one was Bill Campbell, the other was Pete Reeve.

At this point in the story Bull heaved himself slowly, softly up on one arm to listen. He was beginning to get the full sense of the words for the first time. This narrative was like a book done in a commoner language.

Chapter Four

The Summit

The tale halted. To be defeated is one thing; to be forced to confess defeat is another. Uncle Bill determined on the bitterer alternative.

"He made a clean fight," declared Uncle Bill. "First he cussed me out proper. Then he went for his gat and he beat me to the draw. They ain't no disgrace to that. You'll learn pretty soon that anybody might get beaten sooner or later— if he fights enough men. And my gun hung in the leather. Before I got it on him he'd shot me clean through the right shoulder—a placed shot, boys. He wanted to land me there. It tumbled me off my hoss. I rolled away and tried to get to my gun that had fallen on the ground. He shot me ag'in through the leg and stopped me.

Then he got off his hoss and fixed up the wounds. He done a good job, as you seen. 'Bill,' says he, 'you ain't dead; you're worse'n dead. That right arm of yours is going to be stiff the rest of your days. You're a one-armed man from now on, and that one arm is the worst you got.'

"That was why he sent me home alive. To make me live and keep hating him, the same's he'd lived and hated me. But he made a mistake. Pete Reeve is a wise fox, but he made one mistake. He forgot that I might have somebody to send on his trail. He didn't know that I had two boys I'd raised so's they was each better with a gun nor me. He didn't dream of that, curse him! But when you, Harry, or you, Joe, pump the lead into him, shoot him so's he'll live long enough to know who killed him and why!"

As he spoke, there was a quality in his voice that seemed to find the boys in the darkness and point each of them out. "Which of you takes the trail?"

A little silence followed. Bull wondered at it.

"He's gone by way of Johnstown," continued the wounded man. "If one of you cuts across the summit toward Shantung he's pretty sure to cut in across Pete's trail. Which is going to start? Well, you can match for the chance! Because him that comes back with Pete Reeve marked off the slate is a man!"

That chilly little silence made Bull's heart beat. To be called a man, to be praised by stern Bill Campbell—surely these were things to make any one risk death!

"Is that the Pete Reeve," said Harry's voice, "that shot up Mike Rivers over the hill to the Tompkins place, about four year back?"

"That's him. Why?"

Again the silence. Then Bull heard the old man cursing softly—meditatively, one might almost have said.

"Cut across for Johnstown," said Joe slowly, "in a storm like this? They won't be no trails left to find above timber line. It'd be sure death. Listen!"

There was a lull in the wind, and in the breeze that was left, they could hear the whisper of the snow, crushing steadily against the window.

"It's a heavy fall, right enough," declared Harry.

"And this Pete Reeve—why, he's a gunfighter, dad?"

"And what are you?" asked the old man. "Ain't I labored and slaved all my life to make you handy with guns? What for d'you think I wasted all them hours showin' you how to pull a trigger and where to shoot and how to get a gun out of the leather?"

"To kill for meat," suggested Harry.

"Meat, nothing! The kind of meat I mean walks on two feet and fights back."

"Maybe, if we started together—" ventured Joe.

His father broke in: "Bo, I ain't going to send out a pack of men to run down Pete Reeve. He met me single and he fought me clean, and he's going to be pulled down by no pack of yaller dogs! Go one of you alone or else both of you stay here."

He waited, but there was no response. "Is this the way my blood is showing up in my sons? Is this the result of all my trainin'?"

After that there was no more talk. The long silence was not broken by even the sound of breathing until some one began to snore. Then Bull knew that the sleep of the night had settled down.

He lay with his hands folded behind his head, thinking. They were willing enough to go together to do this difficult thing. But had they not lifted together at the stump and failed to do the thing which he had done single-handed? That thought stuck in his memory and would not out. And suppose he, Bull, were to accomplish this great feat and return to the shack? Would not Bill Campbell feel doubly repaid for the living he had furnished for his nephew? More than once the grim old man had cursed the luck that saddled him with a stupid incubus. But the curses would turn to compliments if Bull left this little man, this catlike and dangerous fighter, this Pete Reeve, dead on the trail.

Not that all this was clear in the mind of Bull, but he felt something like a command pushing him on that difficult south trail, through the storm and the snows that would now be piling above timber line. He waited until there was no noise but the snoring of the sleepers and the rush and roar of the wind which continually set something stirring in the room. These sounds served to cover effectually any noises he made as he felt about and made up his small pack. His old canvas coat, his most treasured article of apparel, he took down from the hook where it accumulated dust from month to month. His ancient, secondhand cartridge belt with the aniquated revolver he removed from another hook—he had never been given enough ammunition to become a shot of any quality—and he pushed quickly into the night.

The moment he was through the door, the storm caught him in the face a stinging blow, and the rush of snow chilled his skin. That stinging blow steadied to a blast. It was a tremendous, heavy fall. The wind had scoured the drifts from the clearing and was already banking them around the little house. In the morning, as like as not, the boys would have to dig their way out.

He went straight to the horse shed for his snowshoes that hung on the wall there. Ordinary snowshoes would not endure his ponderous weight, and Uncle Bill Campbell had fashioned these himself, heavy and uncomfortable articles, but capable of enduring the strain.

Fumbling his way down behind the stalls, Bill's roan lashed out at him with savage heels; but Maggie, the old draft horse, whinnied softly, greeting that familiar heavy step. He tied the snowshoes on his back and then stopped for a last word to Maggie. She raised her head and dropped it clumsily on his shoulder. She was among the little, agile mountain ponies what he was among men, and their bulk had rendered each of them more or less helpless. There seemed to be a mute understanding between them, and it was never more apparent than when Maggie whinnied gently in his ear. He stroked her big, bony head, a lump forming in his throat. If the bullets of little Pete Reeve dropped him in some far-off trail the old brokendown horse would be the only living creature that would mourn for him.

Outside, the night and the storm swallowed him at once. Before he had gone fifty feet the house was out of sight. Then, entering the forest of balsam firs, the force of the wind was less-

ened, and he made good time up the first part
of the grade. There would probably be no use
for the snowshoes in this region of broken
shrubbery before he came to the timber line.

He swept on with a lengthening stride. He
knew this part of the country like a book, of
course, and he seldom stumbled, save when he
came out into a clearing and the wind smote at
him from an unexpected angle. In one of these
clearings he stopped and took stock of his position. Far away to the west and the south, the
head of Scalped Mountain was lost in dim,
rushing clouds. He must make for that goal.

Progress became less easy almost at once.
The trees that grew in this elevated region were
not tall enough to act as wind breaks; they were
hardly more than shrubs a great deal of the
time, and merely served to force him into de-
tours around dense hedges. Sometimes, in a
clearing, he found himself staggering to the
knees in a compacted drift of snow; sometimes
an immense sheet of snow was picked up by the
wind and flung in his face like a blanket.

Indeed the cold and the snow were nothing
compared with the wind. It was now reaching
the proportions of a westerly storm of the first
magnitude. Off the towering slopes above, it
came with the chill of the snow and with flying
bits of sand, scooped up from around the base
of trees, or with a shower of twigs. Many a time

he had to throw up his arms across his face before he leaned and thrust on into the teeth of
the blast.

But he was growing accustomed to see
through this veil of snow and thick darkness.
All things were dreamlike in dimness, of course,
but he could make out terrific cloud effects, as
the clouds gushed over the summit and down
the slope a little way like the smoke of enormous guns; and again a pyramid of mist was
like a false mountain before him, a mountain
that took on movement and rushed to over-
whelm him, only to melt away and become simply a shadow among shadows above his head.

Once or twice before the dawn, he rested, not
from weariness perhaps, but from lack of
breath, turning his back to the west and bowing
his head. Walking into the wind it had become
positively difficult to draw breath!

Still it gained power incredibly. Up the side
of Scalped Mountain it was a steady weight
pressing against him rather than a wind. And
now and then, when the weight relaxed, he
stumbled forward on his knees. For there was
now hardly any shelter. He was approaching
the timber line where trees stand as high as a
man and little higher.

Dawn found him at the edge of the tree line.
He flung himself on his face, his head on his
arms, to rest and wait until the treacherous

time of dawn should have passed. While the day grew steadily his heart sank. He needed the rest, but the cold bit into him while he lay extended, and the peril of the summit would be before him for his march of the day. The wind mourned over him as if it anticipated his defeat. Never had there been such wind, he thought. It screamed above him. It dropped away in sudden lulls of more appalling silence. Then, far off, he would hear a wave of the storm begin, wash across a crest, thunder in a canyon, and then break on the timber line with a prolonged and mighty roaring. Those giant approaches made him hold his breath, and when the wave of confusion passed, he found himself often breathless.

Day came. He was on the very verge of the line with a dense fence of stunted trees just before him and the wilderness of snow beyond, sloping up to the crest, outlined in white against the solid gray sky. The Spartans of the forest were around him, fir, pine, spruce, birch, and trembling little aspens up there among the stoutest. All were of one height, clean shaven by the volleys of the wind-driven sand and pebbles that clipped off any treetop that aspired above the mass. In solid numbers was their salvation, and they grew dense as grass, two feet high on the battlefront. They were carved by that wind, for all storms came here out of the west, and the storm face of every tree was denuded of branches. To the east the foliage streamed away. Even in calm weather those trees spoke of storm.

Bull Hunter sat up to put on his snowshoes. It was a white world below him and above. Winter, which a day before had vanished, now came back with a rush off the summits, where its snows were still piled. Again the heart of the big man quaked. Down in the hollow, over that ridge, was the house of the Campbells. They would be getting up now. Joe would be making the fire, and Harry slicing the bacon. It made a cheerful picture to Bull. He could close his eyes and hear the fire snap and see the stove steam with smoke through every fissure before the draft caught in the chimney. From the shed came the neigh of Maggie, calling softly to him.

He shook his head with a groan, stood up, and strode out of the timber into the summit lands. It was a great desert. Never could it be construed as a place for life. Even lichens were almost out of place here, and what folly could lead a man across the shifting snows? But to be called a man, to be admired in silence, to be asked for opinions, to be deferred to—this was a treasure worth any price! He bowed himself to the wind again and made for the summit with the peculiar stride which a man must use with snowshoes.

He dared not slacken his efforts now. The cold had been increasing, and to pause meant peril of freezing. It was a highly electrified air, and the result was a series of maddening mirages. He stumbled over solid rocks where nothing seemed to be in his way; and again what seemed a rock of huge size was nothing at all. Bull discovered that what seemed firm ground beneath him, as he started to round a precipice, might after all be the effect of the mirage.

Added to this was another difficulty. As he wound slowly, about midday, up the last reach, with the summit just above him, the wind carried masses of cloud over the crest and into his face. He walked alternately in a bewildering, driving fog and then in an air made crazy with electricity. Again and again, from one side or the other, he started when the storm boomed and cannonaded down a ravine and then belched out into the open. All this time the babel of the winds overhead never ceased, and the force of the storm cut under him with such violence that he was almost raised from the earth.

Then an unexpected barrier obtruded—a literal mountain of ice was before him. The snow of the recent fall had been whipped away, and the surface of the mountain, here perilously steep, was now sleek and solid with ice. Bull looked gloomily toward the summit so close above him, and the ice glimmered in the dull light. There was only one way to make even the attempt. He sat down, took off his snowshoes, strapped them at his back, and began to work his way up the slope, battering out each foothold with the head of his ax. It was possible to ascend in this manner, but it would be practically impossible to descend.

Once committed to this way, he had either to go on to the summit, or else perish. Working slowly, with little possible muscular exercise to warm him, he began to grow chilled and the wind-driven cold numbed his ears. But, more than that, the wind was now a grim peril, for, from time to time, it swerved and leaped on him heavily from the side. Once, off balance, he looked back at the dazzling slope below him. He would be a shapeless mass of flesh long before he tumbled to the bottom.

Vaguely, as he hewed his footholds and worked his way up, he yearned for the cleverness of Harry or the wit of Joe. What an ally either of them would be! That he was undertaking a task from which either of them would have shrunk in horror never occurred to him. Yonder, beyond the summit, lay his destiny— Johnstown, and this was the way toward it; it was a simple thing to Bull. He could no more vary from his course than a magnetic needle can vary from its pole.

Suddenly he came on a break in the solid face of the ice. Above him was a narrow rift through the ice to the gravel beneath; how it was made, Bull could not guess. But he took advantage of it. Presently he was striding on toward the summit, beating his hands to restore the circulation and gingerly rubbing his ears.

There was a magical change as he reached the summit and sat down behind some rocks to regain his breath and quiet his shaken nerves. The clouds split apart in the zenith; the sun burst through; on both sides the broad mountain billowed away to white lowlands; the air lived with little, brilliant spots of electricity.

It cheered Bull Hunter vastly. The gale, which was tumbling the clouds down the arch of the sky and toward the east, was more mighty than ever, but he put his head down to it confidently and began the descent.

Chapter Five

A Historic Entry

There was more snow on this side, and to travel through it he soon found that he must put on the snowshoes again; but after that the descent was actually restful compared with the labors of the climb. Yonder was the dark streak of timber line again. Far down the valley he watched it curving in and out along the mountainside like a water level. Below was the darkness of the forest where other things lived, and where Bull could live more easily, also. Never had trees seemed such beautiful and friendly things to him.

Once a thought stopped him completely. He

was in a new world. He was seeing everything for the first time. On other days he had gone out with others. Under their guidance, not trusted to undertake an expedition by himself, he looked at nothing until it was pointed out to him, heard nothing that was not first called to his attention. He had always wondered at the acuteness of the senses of all other men. But now, looking on the mountains for himself, he decided, with a start of the heart, that they were beautiful—beautiful and terrible at once, with the reality that he had never found in his books. What leveled spear of a knight, in the pages of romance, could equal the invisible thrust of this wind?

He reached timber line. Looking back, he saw the summit, a brilliant line of white against a blue sky. Again the heart of Bull Hunter leaped. Here was a great treasure that he had taken in with one grasp of the eyes and which he could never lose!

He turned down the valley. Where it swerved out into the lower plain, stood Johnstown, and there he was to cross the flight of Pete Reeve, if Pete were indeed flying. But it was incredible that the man who had struck down Uncle Bill Campbell should flee from any man or number of men.

He had reached the bottom of the narrow valley. A dull noise came down to him from the mountain in the lull of the wind. He looked up.

Far away, miles and miles, near the summit of Scalped Mountain, a snaky form of mist was twisting swiftly down. He looked curiously. The thing grew, traveling with great speed that increased with every moment. It increased—it gained velocity—a snowslide!

He watched it in doubt. It was twisting like a snake down the farther side of the mountain, but, in his experience, slides were as treacherous as serpents. Bull started hastily for a low cliff that stood up from the floor of the valley, clear of the trees.

He had not gone far when the wind fell away to a whisper, and a dull roaring caught his ear. He looked back over his shoulder in alarm. A great wall of white was shooting down the mountainside. The little slide of surface snow, which had twisted across the surface of the old snows of the winter, had been gaining in weight, in momentum, picking up claws of shrubbery, teeth of stone, and eating through layer after layer of the old snow, packed hard as ice. Now it was a roaring mass with a front steadily increasing in height, and far away in the rear it tossed up a tail of snow dust, a flying mist that gave Bull an impression of speed greater than the main wall of the snow itself.

The noise grew amazingly, and, coming in range of the opposite wall of the valley, a low and steadily increasing thunder poured into the ears of Bull. It was a fascinating thing to watch, and at this distance to the side he was quite safe. But in the very moment that he reached this decision, the front of the slide smashed with a noise like volleyed cannon against the side of a hill, tossed immense arms of white in the air, floundered, and then veered with the speed of an express train rounding a curve and rocked away down the slope straight for Bull. Turned cold with dread, he saw it hit timber line with a great crashing, and the dark forms of the trees were dashed up by the running mass of stones and then swallowed in the boiling front of the slide.

He waited to see no more, but dashed on for the saving cliff. Once his back was turned it seemed that the slide gained speed. The immense roaring literally leaped on him from behind, and in the roar, his senses were drowned. He could feel his knees weaken and buckle, but the cliff, now just before him, gave him fresh strength. But was the cliff high enough? He hurried up to higher ground and flung himself prostrate. The front of the slide was cutting down the heavily forested slope as though the trees were blades of grass before a keen scythe. The noise passed all description.

Once he thought the mass was changing direction. It put out a massive arm to the left, licked down five hundred trees at a gulp, and then, smashing its fist into a hillside, flung back into the valley floor, tossing the great trees in its top and poured straight at him. He watched it in one of those dazes during which one sees everything. The whole body came like water down a chute, but one part of the front wall spilled out ahead and then another, and then the top, overtaking the rest, toppled crashing to the bottom. And so it rushed out of sight beneath the cliff. But would it wash over the top?

The first answer was an impact that shook the ground under him, and then he heard a noise like a huge ripping explosion. A dozen lofty geysers of snow streamed up into the air, dazzling against the sun, misty at the edges of each column, whose center was solid tons and tons of snow. Old pines and spruces, their branches shaved away in the tumult of the slide, were picked up and hurled like javelins over the cliff; a shower of fragments beat on the body of Bull; and then the main mass of snow washed up over the edge of the cliff in a great mound, and the slide was ended.

He crawled slowly back to his feet. Far up the mountainside, beginning in a point, the track of the slide swept down in a broadening scar, black and raw, across forest and snow. Far down the valley the last echoes of thunder were passing away to a murmur, and the valley floor, beneath the cliff, was a mass of snow and tree trunks.

Bull took off the snowshoes and climbed along the valley wall until he could descend to the clear floor beneath him. Then he headed down toward Johnstown.

It was well past midday when he escaped the slide; it was the beginning of night when, at the conclusion of that first heroic march, he reached Johnstown. With hunger his stomach cleaved to his back, and his knees were weak with the labor.

Stamping through the snow to the hotel he asked the idlers around the stove: "Has any of you gents seen a man named Pete Reeve pass through this town?"

They looked at him in amazement. He had closed the door behind him, and now, with his battered hat pushed high on his head, he seemed taller than the entrance—taller and as wide, a mountain of a man. The efforts of the march had collected a continual frown on his forehead, and as he peered about from face to face, no one for a moment was able to answer, but each looked to his companion.

It was the proprietor who answered finally. Talk was his commercial medium and staff of life. "What sort of a looking man, Captain?"

Bull blinked at him. He was not used to honorary epithets such as this, and he searched the face of the proprietor carefully to detect mockery. To his surprise the other showed signs of what Bull dimly recognized as fear. Fear of him—of Bull Hunter!

"The way you look at me," said the other and laughed uneasily, "I figure it's pretty lucky that I ain't this here Pete Reeve. That so, boys?"

The boys joined in the laughter, but they kept it subdued, their eyes upon the giant at the door. He was leaning against the wall, and the sight of his outspread hand was far from reassuring.

But Bull went on to describe his man. "Not very big; hands like the claws of a bird's; iron-gray hair; quick ways." That was Uncle Bill's description.

"Sure he's been here," said the owner. "I recognized him right off. He was through about dusk. He came over the mountains and just got past the summit, he said, before the storm hit. Lucky, eh?" He looked at the battered coat of Bull. "Kind of appears like you mightn't of been so lucky?"

"Me?" asked Bull gently. "Nope. I was at timber line on the other side about daybreak today."

There was a sudden and chilly silence; men looked at one another. Obviously no man could have traveled that distance between dawn and dark, but it was as well not to express disbelief to a man who could tell a lie as big as his body.

"I got to eat," said Bull.

The proprietor jumped out of his chair. "I can fix you up, son."

He led the way, Bull following with his enormous strides, and, as the floor creaked under him, the eyes of the others jerked after him, stride by stride. It was beginning to seem possible that this man had done what he said he had done. When the door slammed behind him and his steps went creaking through the room beyond, a mutter of a hum arose around the stove.

As a matter of fact it was the beginning of the great legend that was finally to bulk around the name of the big man. And it was fitting that the huge figure of Bull Hunter should have come upon the attention of men in this way, descending out of the storm and the mountains.

That he had done something historic was far from the mind of Bull as he stalked into the dining room.

"You sit right down here," his host was saying, placing a chair at the table.

Bull tried the chair with his hand. It groaned and squeaked under the weight. "Chairs don't seem to be made for me," he said simply. "Besides I'm more used to sitting on the floor." He dropped to the floor accordingly, with the effect of a small earthquake. The proprietor stared,

63

but he swallowed his astonishment. "What you'd like to eat is something hearty, I figure."

"What you got?" said Bull.

"Well, Mrs. Jarney come in this morning with a dozen fresh eggs. Got some prime bacon, too, and some jerky and—"

"That dozen eggs," said Bull thoughtfully, "will start me, and then a platter of bacon, and you might mix up a bowl of flapjacks. You ain't got a quart or so of canned milk, partner?"

Mine host could only nod, for he dared not trust his voice. Fleeing to the kitchen he repeated the prodigious order to his wife. Then he circled by a back way and communicated the tidings to the "boys" around the stove.

"A couple of dozen eggs, he says to me, and a few pounds of beef and three or four quarts of milk and a bowl of flapjacks and a platter of bacon," was the way the second version of that historic order for food came to the idlers.

Half a dozen of the men risked the cold and the wind to steal around to the side of the house and peer through the window at the huge, bunched figure that sat on the floor. They found him with his chin dropped upon the burly fist and a frown on his forehead, for Bull was thinking.

He would have been glad to have found Pete Reeve in Johnstown and have the matter over with. But, after all, it was beginning to occur to him that it might not be wise to kill the man in the presence of other people. They might attempt to correct him with the assistance of a rope and a limb of a tree. Somewhere he must cut in ahead of this Reeve and start out at him if possible. As for his ability to keep pace with a horse, he had no doubt that he could do it fairly well. More than once he had gone out on foot, while Harry and Joe rode, and he had pressed the little ponies, bearing their riders slowly up and down the slopes, to keep pace with him. On the level, of course, it was a different matter, but in broken country he more than kept up.

"Have you got a grudge agin' Reeve?" asked the host, as he brought in the fried eggs.

"Maybe," admitted Bull, and instantly he began to attack the food.

Mine host watched with a growing awe. No Chinook ever ate snow as this hungry giant melted food to nothingness. He came back with the first stack of flapjacks and bacon and more questions. "But I'd think that a gent like you'd be pretty careful about tangling with Pete Reeve—him being so handy with a gun and you such a tolerable big target."

"I've figured that all out," said Bull calmly. "But they's so much of me to kill that I don't figure one bullet could do the work. Do you?"

The eyes of the proprietor grew large. He

swallowed, and before he could answer Bull continued in the exposition of his theory. "Before he shoots the next shot, maybe I can get my hands on him."

"You going to fight him bare hands agin' a gun?"

"You see," said Bull apologetically, "I ain't much good with a gun, but I feel sort of curious about what would happen if I got my grip on a man."

And that was the foundation on which another section of the Bull Hunter legend was built.

Chapter Six

The Sheriff's Bear

The bed on which Bull Hunter reposed his bulk that night was not the cot to which he was shown by his host. One glance at the spindling wooden legs of the canvas-bottomed cot was enough for Bull, and having wrapped himself in the covers he lay down on the floor and was instantly asleep.

While it was still dark, he wakened out of a dream in which Pete Reeve seemed to be riding far—far away on the rim of the world. Ten minutes later Bull was on the trail out of Johnstown. There was only one trail for a horseman south of Johnstown, and that trail followed the windings of the valley. Bull planned to push across the ragged peaks of the Little Cloudy Mountains and head off the fugitive at Glenn Crossing.

Two days of stern labor went into that next burst. He followed the cold stars by night and the easy landmarks by day, and for food he had the stock of raisins he had bought at Johnstown. He came out of the heights and dropped down into Glenn Crossing in the gloom of the second evening. But raisins are meager support for such a bulk as that of Bull Hunter. It was a gaunt-faced giant who looked in at the door of the blacksmith shop where the blacksmith was working late. The mechanic looked up with a start at the deep voice of the stranger, but he managed to stammer forth his tidings. Such a man as Pete Reeve had indeed been in Glenn Crossing, but he had gone on at the very verge of day and night.

Bull Hunter set his teeth, for there was no longer a possibility of cutting off Pete Reeve by crossing country. The immense labors of the last three days had merely served to put him on the heels of the horseman, and now he must follow straight down country and attempt to match his long legs against the speed of a fine horse. He drew a deep breath and plunged into the night out of Glenn Crossing, on the south trail. At least he would make one short, stiff march before the weariness overtook him.

That weariness clouded his brain ten miles out. He built a fire in a cover of pines and slept beside it. Before dawn he was up and out again. In the first gray of the daylight he reached a little store at a crossroad, and here he paused for breakfast. A tousled girl, rubbing the sleep out of her eyes, served him in the kitchen. The first glimpse of the hollow cheeks and the unshaven face of Bull Hunter quite awakened her. Bull could feel her watching him as she glided about the room. He sunk his head between his shoulders and glared down at the table. No doubt she would begin to gibe at him before long. Most women did. He prepared himself to meet with patience that incredible sting and penetrating hurt of a woman's mockery.

But there was no mockery forthcoming. The sun was still not up when he paid his bill and hastened to the door of the old building. Quick footsteps followed him, a hand touched his shoulders, and he turned and looked suspiciously down into the face of the girl. It was a frightened face, he thought, and very pretty. At some interval between the time when he first saw her and the present, she had found time to rearrange her hair and make it smooth. Color was pulsing in her cheeks.

"Stranger," she said softly, "what are you running away from?"

The question slowly penetrated the mind of Bull; he was still bewildered by the change in her—something electric, to be felt rather than noted with the eye.

"They ain't any reason for hurrying on," she urged. "I—I can hide you, easy. Nobody could find you where I'll put you, and there you can rest up. You must be tolerable tired."

There was no doubt about it. There was kindness as well as anxiety in her voice. For the second time in his entire life, Bull decided that a woman could be something more than an annoyance. She was placing a value on him, just as Jessie, three days before, had placed a value on him; and it disturbed Bull. For so many years he had been mocked and scorned by his uncle and cousins that deep in his mind was graved the certainty that he was useless. He decided to hurry on before the girl found out the truth.

"I can still walk," he said, "and, while I can walk, I got to go south. But—you gimme heart, lady. You gimme a pile of heart to keep going. Maybe"—he paused, uncertain what to say next, and yet obviously she expected something more—"I'll get a chance to come back this way, and if I do, I'll see you! You can lay to that—I'll see you!"

He was gone before she could answer, and he was wondering why she had looked down with that sudden color and that queer, pleased smile. It would be long before Bull understood, but, even without understanding, he found that his heart was lighter and an odd warmth suffused him.

The rising of the sun found him in the pale desert with the magic of the hills growing distant behind him, and he settled to a different step through the thin sand—a short, choppy step. His weight was against him here, but it would be even a greater disadvantage to a horseman, and with this in mind, he pressed steadily south.

Every day on that south trail was like a year in the life of Bull. Heat and thirst wasted him, the constant labor of the march hardened his muscles, and he got that forward look about his eyes, which comes with shadows under the lids and a constant frown on the forehead. It was long afterward that men checked up his march from date to date and discovered that the distance, between the shack of Bill Campbell and Halstead in the south, was one hundred and fifty miles over bitter mountains and burning desert; and that Bull Hunter had made the distance in five days.

All this was learned and verified later when Bull was a legend. When he strode into Halstead on that late afternoon no one had ever heard of the man out of the mountains. He was simply an oddity in a country where oddities draw small attention.

Yet a rumor advanced before Bull. A child, playing in the incredible heat of the sun, saw the dusty giant heaving in the distance and ran to its mother, frightened, and the worn-faced mother came to the porch and shaded her eyes to look. She passed on the word with a call that traveled from house to house. So that, when Bull entered the long, irregular street of Halstead, he found it lined on either side by children, old men, women. It was almost as though they had heard of the thing he had come to do and were there to watch.

Bull shrank from their eyes. He would far rather have slipped around the back of the village and gone toward its center unobserved. A pair of staring eyes to Bull was like the pointing of a loaded gun. He put unspoken sentences upon every tongue, and the sentences were those he had heard so often from his uncle and his uncle's boys:

"Too big to be any good."

"Bull's got the size of a hoss, and as a hoss he'd do pretty well, but he ain't no account as a man."

His life had been paved with such burning remarks as these. Many an evening had been a long agony to him as the three sat about and baited him. He hurried down the street, the pulverized sand squirting up about his heavy boots and drifting in a mist behind him. When he was gone an old man came out and measured those great strides with his eye and then stretched his legs vainly to cover the same marks. But this, of course, Bull did not see, and he would not have understood it, had he seen, except as a mockery.

He paused in front of the hotel veranda, an awful figure to behold. His canvas coat was rolled and tied behind his sweating shoulders; his short sleeves had bothered him and they were now cut off at the elbow and exposed the sun-blackened forearms; his overalls streamed in rags over his scarred boots. He pushed the battered hat far back on his head and looked at the silent, attentive line of idlers who sat on the veranda.

"Excuse me, gents," he said mildly. "But maybe one of you might know of a little gent with iron-gray hair and a thin face and quick ways of acting and little, thin hands." He illustrated his meaning by extending his own huge paw. "His name is Pete Reeve."

That name caused a sharp shifting of glances, not at Bull, but from man to man. A tall fellow rose. He advanced with his thumbs hooked importantly in the armholes of his vest and braced his legs apart as he faced Bull. The elevation of the veranda floor raised him so that he was actully some inches above the head of his interlocutor, and the tall man was deeply grateful for that advantage. He was, in truth, a little vain of his own height, and to have to look up to any one irritated him beyond words. Having established his own superior position, he looked the giant over from head to foot. He kept one eye steadily on Bull, as though afraid that the big man might dodge out of sight and elude him.

"And what might you have to do with Pete Reeve?" he asked. "Mightn't you be a partner of Pete's? Kind of looks like you was following him sort of eager, friend."

While this question was being asked, Bull saw that the line of idlers settled forward in their chairs to hear the answer. It puzzled him. For some mysterious reason these men disapproved of any one who was intimately acquainted with Pete Reeve, it seemed. He looked blandly upon the tall man.

"I never seen Pete Reeve," said Bull apologetically.

"Eh? Yet you're follerin' him hotfoot?"

"I was aiming to see him, you know," answered Bull.

The tall man regarded him with eyes that began to twinkle beneath his frown. Then he jerked his head aside and cast at his audience a prodigious wink. The cloudy eyes of Bull had assured him that he had to do with a simpleton, and he was inviting the others in on the game.

"You never seen him?" he asked gruffly, turning back to Bull. "You expect me to believe talk like that? Young man, d'you know who I am?"

"I dunno," murmured Bull, overawed and drawing back a pace.

The action drew a chuckle from the crowd. Some of the idlers even rose and sauntered to the edge of the veranda, the better to see the baiting of the giant. His prodigious size made his timidity the more amusing.

"You dunno, eh?" asked the other. "Well, son, I'm Sheriff Bill Anderson!" He waited to see the effect of this portentous announcement.

"I never heard tell of any Sheriff Bill Anderson," said Bull in the same mild voice.

The sheriff gasped. The idlers hastily veiled their mouths with much coughing and clearing of the throat. It seemed that the tables had been subtly turned upon the sheriff.

"You!" exclaimed the sheriff, extending a bony arm. "I got to tell you, partner, that I'm a pile suspicious. I'm suspicious of anybody that's a friend of Pete Reeve. How long have you knowed him?"

Bull was very anxious to pacify the tall man. He shifted his weight to the other foot. "Something less'n nothing," he hastened to explain. "I ain't never seen him."

"And why d'you want to see him? What d'you know about him?"

It flashed through the mind of Bull that it would be useless to tell what he knew of Pete Reeve. Obviously nobody would believe what he could tell of how Reeve had met and shot down Uncle Bill Campbell. For Bill Campbell was a historic figure as a fighter in the mountain regions, and surely his fame must be bright even at this distance from his home. That he could have walked beyond the sphere of Campbell's fame in five days never occurred to Bull Hunter.

"I dunno nothing good," he confessed.

There was a change in the sheriff. He descended from the floor of the veranda with a stiff-legged hop and took Bull by the arm, leading him down the street.

"Son," he said earnestly, walking down the street with Bull, "d'you know anything agin' this Pete Reeve? I want to know because I got Pete behind the bars for murder!"

He made a pause, stopped by the sudden halt of Bull.

"Murder?" asked Bull.

"Murder—regular murder—something he'll hang for. And if you got any inside information that I can use agin' him, why I'll use it and I'll be mighty grateful for it! You see everybody knows Pete Reeve. Everybody knows that, for all these years, he's been going around killing and maiming men, and nobody has been able to bring him up for anything worse'n self-defense. But now I think I got him to rights, and I want to hang him for it, stranger, partly because it'd be a feather in my cap, and partly because it'd be doing a favor for every good, law-abiding citizen in these parts. So do what you can to help me, stranger, and I'll see that your time ain't wasted."

There was something very wheedling and insinuating about all this talk. It troubled Bull. His strangely obscure life had left him a child in many important respects, and he had a child's instinctive knowledge of the mental processes of others. In this case he felt a profound distrust. There was something wrong about this sheriff, his instincts told him—something gravely wrong. He disliked the man who had started to ridicule him before many men and was now so confidential, asking his help.

"Sheriff Anderson," he said, "may I see this Reeve?"

"Come right along with me, son. I ain't pressing you for what you know. But it may be a thing that'll help me to hang Reeve. And if it is, I'll need to know it. Understand? Public benefit—that's what I'm after. Come along with me and you can see if Reeve's the man you're after."

They crossed the street through a little maelstrom of fine dust which a wind circle had picked up, and the sheriff led Bull into the jail.

They crossed the tawdry little outer room with its warped floor creaking under the tread of Bull Hunter. Next they came face to face with a cage of steel bars, and behind it was a little gray man on a bunk. He sat up and peered at them from beneath bushy brows, a thin-faced man, extremely agile. Even in sitting up, one caught many possibilities of catlike speed of action.

Bull knew at once that this was the man he sought. He stood close to the bars, grasping one in each great hand, and, with his face pressed against the steel, he peered at Pete Reeve. The other was very calm.

"Howdy, sheriff," he said. "Bringing on another one to look over your bear?"

Chapter Seven

Streaked Stones

The prisoner's good humor impressed Bull immensely. Here was a man talking commonplaces in the face of death. A greater man than Uncle Bill, he felt at once—a far greater man. It was impossible to conceive of that keen, sharp eye and that clawlike hand sending a bullet far from the center of the target.

He gave his eyes long sight of that face, and then turned from the bars and went out with the sheriff.

"Is that your man?" asked the sheriff.

"I dunno," said Bull, fencing for time as they stood in front of the jail. "What'd he do?"

"You mean why he's in jail? I'll tell you that, son, but first I want to know what you got agin' him—and your proofs—mostly your proofs!"

The distaste which Bull had felt for the sheriff from the first now became overpowering. That he should be the means of bringing that terrible and active little man to an end seemed, as a matter of fact, absurd. Guile must have played a part in that capture.

Suppose he were to tell the sheriff about the shooting of Uncle Bill? That would be enough to convince men that Pete Reeve was capable of murder, for the shooting of Uncle Bill had been worse than murder. It spared the life and ruined it at the same time. But suppose he added his evidence and allowed the law to take its course with Pete Reeve? Where would be his own reward for his long march south and all the pain of the travel and the crossing of the mountains at the peril of his life? There would be nothing but scorn from Uncle Bill when he returned, and not that moment of praise for which he yearned. To gain that great end he must kill Pete Reeve, but not by the aid of the law.

"I dunno," he said to the sheriff who waited impatiently. "I figure that what I know wouldn't be no good to you."

The sheriff snorted. "You been letting me waste all this time on you?" he asked Bull. "Why didn't you tell me that in the first place?"

Bull scratched his head in perplexity. But as he raised the great arm and put his hand behind his head, the sheriff winced back a little. "I'm sorry," said Bull.

The sheriff dismissed him with a grunt of disgust, and strode off.

Bull started out to find information. This idea was growing slowly in his mind. He must kill Pete Reeve, and to accomplish that great end he must first free him from the jail. He went back to the hotel and went into the kitchen to find food. The proprietor himself came back to serve him. He was a pudgy little man with a dignified pointed beard of which he was inordinately proud.

"It's between times for meals," he declared, "but you being the biggest man that ever come into the hotel, I'll make an exception." And he began to hunt through the cupboard for cold meat.

"I seen Pete Reeve," began Bull bluntly. "How come he's in jail?"

"Him?" asked the other. "Ain't you heard?"

"No."

The little man sighed with pleasure; he had given up hope of finding a new listener for that oft-told tale. "It happened last night," he confided. "Along late in the afternoon in rides Johnny Strange. He tells us he was out to Dan Armstrong's place when, about noon, a little

81

gray-headed man, that give the name of Pete Reeve, came in and asked for chow. Of course Johnny Strange pricks up his ears when he hears the name. We all heard about Pete Reeve, off and on, as about the slickest gunman that the ranges ever turned out. So he looks Pete over and wonders at finding such a little man."

The proprietor drew himself up to his full height. "He didn't know that size don't make the man! Well, Armstrong trotted out some chuck for Reeve, and after Pete had eaten, Johnny Strange suggested a game. They sat in at three-handed stud poker.

"Things went along pretty good for Johnny. He made a considerable winning. Then it come late in the afternoon, and he seen he'd have to be getting back home. He offered to bet everything he'd won, double or nothing, and when the boys didn't want to do that, it give him a clean hand to stand up and get out. He got up and said good-by and hung around a while to see how the next hands went. So far as he could make out, Pete Reeve was losing pretty steady. Then he come on in.

"Well, when Johnny Strange told about Pete being out there, Sheriff Anderson was in the room and he rises up.

" 'Don't look good to me,' he says. 'If a gun-fighter is losing money, most like he'll fight to win it back. Maybe I'll go out and look that game over.'

"And saying that he slopes out of the room.

"Well, none of us took much stock in the sheriff going out to take care of Armstrong. You see Armstrong was the old sheriff, and he give Anderson a pretty stiff run for his money last election. They both been spending most of their time and energy the last few years hating each other. When one of 'em is in office the other goes around saying that the gent that has the plum is a crook; and then Anderson goes out, and Armstrong comes in, and Anderson says the same thing about Armstrong. Take 'em general and they always had the boys worried when they was together, for fear of a gunfight and bullets flying. And so, when Anderson stands up and says he's going out to see that Reeve don't do no harm to Armstrong, we all sat back and kind of laughed.

"But we laughed at the wrong thing. Long about an hour or so after dark we hear two men come walking up on the veranda, and one of 'em we knowed by the sound was the sheriff."

"How could you tell by the sound?" asked Bull innocently.

"Well, you see the sheriff always wears steel rims on his heels like he was a horse. He's kind of close with his money is old Anderson, I'll tell a man! We hear the ring of them heels on the porch, and pretty soon in comes the sheriff, herding a gent in ahead of him. And who do d'you think that gent was? It was Reeve! Yes, sir, the old sheriff had stepped out and grabbed his man. He wasn't there quick enough to stop the killing of Armstrong, but he got there fast enough to nab Reeve. Seems that, when he was riding up to the house, he heard a shot fired, and then he seen a man run out of the house and jump on his hoss, and the sheriff didn't stop to ask no questions. He just out with his gat and drills the gent's hoss. And while Reeve was struggling on the ground, with the hoss flopping around and dying, the sheriff runs up and sticks the irons on Reeve. Then he goes into the house and finds Armstrong lying shot through the heart. Clear as day! Reeve loses a lot of money, and when it comes to a pinch he hates to see that money gone when he could get it back for the price of one slug. So he outs with his gun and shoots Armstrong. And the worst part of it was that Armstrong didn't have no gun on at the time. The sheriff found Armstrong's gun hanging on the wall along with his cartridge belt. Yep, it was plain murder, and Pete Reeve'll hang as high as the sky—and a good thing, too!"

This story was a shock to Bull for a reason that would not have affected most men. That a man who had had the courage to stand up and face Uncle Bill in a fair duel should have been so cowardly, so venomous as to take a mean advantage of a gambling companion seemed to Bull altogether too strange to be reasonable. Certainly, if he had had a difference with this fellow, thought Bull, Pete Reeve was the man to let the other use his own weapons before he fought. But to shoot him down across a table, unwarned—this was too much to believe! And yet it was the truth, and Pete Reeve was to hang for it.

The big man sat shaking his head. "And they found the money on Pete Reeve?" he asked gloomily. "They found the money he took off this Armstrong?"

"There's the funny part of the yarn," said the proprietor glibly. "Pete had the nerve to shoot the gent down in cold blood, but when he seen him fall he lost his nerve. He didn't wait to grab the money, but ran out and jumped on his hoss and tried to get away. So there you are. But it pretty often happens that way! Take the oldest gunfighter in the world, and, if his stomach ain't resting just right, it sort of upsets him to see a crimson stain. I seen it happen that way with the worst of 'em, and in the old days they used to be a rough crowd in my barroom. They don't turn out that style of gent no more!" He sighed as his mind flickered back into the heroic past.

"And Reeve—he admits he done the killing?" Bull asked hopelessly.

"Him? Nope, he's too foxy for that. But the only story he told was so foolish that we laughed at him, and he ain't had the nerve to try to bluff us ever since. He says that he was sitting peaceable with Armstrong when all at once without no warning, they was a shot from the window—the east window, I remember he was particular to say—and Armstrong dropped forward on the table, shot through the heart.

"Reeve says that he didn't wait to ask no questions. He blew the candle out, and having got the darkness on his side, he made a jump through the door and got onto his hoss. He says that he wanted to break away to the trees and try to get a shot at the murderer from cover, but the minute he got onto his hoss, he had his hoss shot from under him."

"Was they any shots fired then?"

"Yep; Reeve says that he fired a couple of times when he fell. But the sheriff says that Reeve only fired once, as his hoss was falling, and that the other shot, that was found fired out of Reeve's gun, was fired into the heart of Armstrong. Oh, they ain't any doubt about it. All Reeve has got is a cock-and-bull yarn that would make a fool laugh!"

Although Bull had been many times assured by his uncle and his cousins that he was a fool of the first magnitude, he was in no mood for laughter. Somewhere in the tale there was something wrong, for his mind refused to conjure up the picture of Reeve pulling his gun and shooting across the table into the breast of a helpless, unwarned man. That would not be the method of a man who could stand up to Uncle Bill. That would not be the method of the man who had sat up on his bunk and looked so calmly into the face of the sheriff.

Bull stood up and dragged his hat firmly over his eyes. "I'd kind of like to see the place where that shooting was done," he declared.

"You got lots of time before night," said the proprietor. "Ain't more'n a mile and a half out the north trail. Take that path right out there, and you can ride out inside of five minutes."

There was no horse for Bull Hunter to ride. But, having thanked his host, he stepped out into the cooler sunshine of the late afternoon.

The trail led through scattering groves of cotton-wood most of the way, for it was bottom land, partially flooded in the winter season of rain, and, even in the driest and hottest part of the summer, marshy in places. He followed the twisting little trail through spots of shadow and stretches of open sky until he reached the shack which was obviously that of the dead Armstrong.

The moment he entered the little cabin he received proof positive.

The furniture had not apparently been disturbed since the shooting. The table still leaned crazily, as though it had not recovered from a violent shock on one side. One chair was overturned. A box had been smashed to splinters, probably by having some one put a foot through it.

Bull examined the deal table. Across the center of it there was a dark stain, and on the farther side, two hands were printed distinctly into the wood, in the same dull color. The whole scene rose revoltingly distinct in the mind of Bull.

Here sat Dan Armstrong playing his cheerful game, laughing and jesting, because forsooth he was the winner. And there, on the opposite side of the table, sat Pete Reeve, the guest in the house of his host, growing darker and darker as the money was transferred from his pocket to the pocket of the jovial Armstrong. Then, a sudden taking of offense at some harmless jest, the cold flash of steel as Reeve leaned and jumped to his feet, and then the explosion of the revolver, with Armstrong settling slowly, limply forward on the table. There he lay with a stream pouring across the table from the death wound, his helpless arms outstretched on the wood.

Then Reeve, panic-stricken, perhaps with a

sudden stirring of remorse, started for the door, struck the box on his way, smashing it to bits, and as soon as he got outside, leaped for his horse. Luckily retribution had overtaken the murderer in the very moment of escape. Bull Hunter sighed. Never had the strength of the arm of the law been so vividly brought home to him as by this incident. Suppose that he had fulfilled his purpose and killed Reeve? Would not the law have reached for him in the same fashion and taken and crushed him?

He shuddered, and looking up from his broodings, he glanced through the opposite window and saw that the woods were growing dark in that direction. Night was approaching, and, with the feeling of night, there was a ghostly sense of death, as though the spirit of the dead man were returning to his old home. On the other side of the house, however, the woods showed brighter. This was the east window—the east window through which Reeve declared that the shot had been fired.

Bull shook his head. He stepped out of the cabin and looked about. It was a prosperous little stretch of meadow, cleared into the cottonwoods and reclaiming part of the marsh land—all very rich soil, as one could see at a glance. There was a field which had been recently upturned by the plow, perhaps the work of yesterday. The furrows were still black, still not dried out by the sun. Today would have been the time for harrowing, but that work was indefinitely postponed by the grim visitor. No doubt this Armstrong was an industrious man. The sense of a wasted life was brought home to Bull; a bullet hand ended it all!

Absentmindedly he passed around the side of the house and started for the east window through which Reeve had said that the bullet was fired, but he shook his head at once.

On the east side the house leaned against a mass of white stone. It rose high, rough, ragged. Certainly a man stalking a house to fire a shot would never come up to it from this side! His own words were convicting Reeve of the murder!

Still he continued to clamber over the stones until he stood by the window. To be sure, if a man stood there, he could easily have fired into the room and into the breast of a man sitting on the far side of the table. Armstrong was found there. Bull looked down to his feet as a thoughtful man will do, and there, very clearly marked against the white of the stone, he saw a dark streak—two of them, side by side.

He bent and looked at them. Then he rubbed the places with his finger tips and examined the skin. A stain had come away from the rock. It was as if the rocks had been rubbed with lead or a soft iron. And then, strangely, into the mind of Bull came the memory of what the hotelman had said of the sheriff's iron-shod heels.

The sheriff had gone for many a year hating Armstrong. The truth rushed over the brain of the big man. What a chance for a crafty mind! To kill his enemy and place the blame on the shoulders of one already known to be a man-killer! Bull Hunter leaped from the rocks and started back for the town with long, ground-devouring strides.

Chapter Eight

A Conference

There were two reasons for the happiness which lightened the step of Bull Hunter as he strode back for the town. In the first place he saw a hope of liberating Reeve from jail and accomplishing his own mission of killing the man. In the second place he felt a peculiar joy at the thought of freeing such a man from the imputation of a cowardly murder.

Yet he had small grounds for his hopes. Two little dark marks on the white, friable stone, marks that the first small shower of rain would wash away, marks that the first keen sand storm would rub off—these were his only proofs. And with these to free one man from danger of the rope and place the head of another under the noose—it was a task to try the resources of a cleverer man than Bull.

Indeed, the high spirits of Bull in some measure left him as he drew nearer and nearer to the village. How could he convict the sheriff? How, with his clumsy wits and his clumsy tongue, could he bring the truth to light? Had he possessed the keen eye of his uncle he felt that a single glance would have made the guilt stand up in the face of Anderson. But his own eyes, alas, were dull and clouded.

Thoughtfully, with bowed head, he held his course. A strange picture, surely, this man who so devoutly wished to free another from the danger of the law in order that he might take a life into his own hands. But the contrast did not strike home to Bull. To him everything that he did was as clear as day. But how to go to work? If the man were like himself it would be an easy matter. More than once he remembered how his cousins had shifted the blame for their own boyish pranks upon him. In the presence of their father they would accuse Bull with a well-planned lie, and the very fact that he had been accused made Bull blush and hang his head. Before he could be heard in his own behalf the cruel eye of his uncle had grown stern, and Bull was condemned as a culprit.

"The only time you show any sense," his uncle had said more than once, "is when you want to do something you hadn't ought to do!"

Steadily through the years he had served as a scapegoat for his cousins. They set a certain value upon him for his use in this respect. Ah, if only he had that keen, embarrassing eye of Bill Campbell with which to pierce to the guilty heart of the sheriff and make him speak! The eye of his uncle was like the eye of a crowd. It was an audience in itself and condemned or praised with the strength of numbers.

It was this thought of numbers that brought the clue to a possible solution to Bull Hunter. When it came to him he stopped short in the road, threw back his head and laughed.

"And what's all the celebration about?" asked a voice behind him.

He turned and found Sheriff Anderson on his horse directly behind him. The soft loam of the trail had covered the sound of the sheriff's approach. Bull blushed with a sudden sense of shame. Moreover, the sheriff seemed unapproachably stern and dignified. He sat erect in the saddle, a cavalier figure with his long, well-drilled mustaches.

"I dunno," said Bull vaguely, pushing his hat back to scratch his thatch of blond hair. "I didn't know I was celebrating, particular."

The sheriff watched him with small, evil eyes.

"You been snooping around, son," he said coldly. "And we folks in this part, we don't like snoopers. Understand?"

"No," said Bull frankly, "I don't exactly figure what you mean." Then he dropped his hand to his hip.

"Git your hand off that gun!" said the sheriff, his own weapon flashing instantly in the light.

It had been a move like lightning. Its speed stunned and baffled Bull Hunter. Something cold formed in his throat, choking him, and he obediently drew his hand away. He did more. He threw both immense arms above his head and stood gaping at the sheriff.

The latter eyed him for a moment with stern amusement, and then he shoved the gun back into its holster. "I guess they ain't much harm in you," he said more to himself than to Bull. "But I hate a snooper worse than I do a rat. You can take them arms down."

Bull lowered them cautiously.

"You hear me talk?" asked the sheriff.

"I hear," said Bull obediently.

"I don't like snoopers. Which means that I don't like you none too well. Besides, who in thunder are you? A wanderin' vagrant you look to me, and we got a law agin' vagrants. You amble along on your trail pretty pronto, and no harm'll come to you. But if you're around town tomorrow—well, you've heard me talk!"

It was very familiar talk to Bull; not the words, but the commanding and contemptuous tone in which they were spoken. Crestfallen, he submitted. Of one thing he must make sure; that no harm befell him before he faced Pete Reeve and Pete Reeve's gun. Then he could only pray for courage to attack. But the effect of the sheriff's little gun play entirely disheartened Bull at the prospect of facing Pete.

With a noncommittal rejoinder he started down the road, and the sheriff put the spurs to his horse and plunged by at a full gallop, flinging the dust back into the face of the big man. Bull wiped it out of his eyes and went on gloomily. He had been trodden upon in spirit once more. But, after all, that was so old a story that it made little difference. It convinced him, however, of one thing; he could never do anything with the sheriff man to man. Certainly he would need the help of a crowd before he faced the tall man and his cavalier mustaches.

He waited until after the supper at the hotel. It was a miserable meal for Bull; he had already eaten, and he could not find a way of refusing the invitation of the proprietor to sit down again. Seated at the end of the long table he looked miserably up and down it. Nobody had a look for him except one of contempt. The sheriff, it seemed, had spread a story around about his lack of spirit, and if Bull remained long in the village, he would be treated with little more respect than he had been in the house of his uncle. Even now they held him in contempt. They could not understand, for instance, why he sat so far forward. He was resting most of his weight on his legs, for fear of the weakness of the chair under his full bulk. But that very bulk made them whisper their jokes and insults to one another.

When the long nightmare of that meal was ended, Bull began making his rounds. He had chosen his men. Every man he picked was sharp-eyed like Uncle Bill Campbell. They were the men whose in-looking eyes would baffle the sheriff; they were the men capable of suspicions, and such men Bull needed—not dull-glancing people like himself.

He went first to the proprietor of the hotel. "I got something to say to the sheriff," he declared. "And I want to have a few important gents around town to be there to listen and hear what I got to say. I wonder could you be handy?"

He was surprised at the avidity with which his invitation was accepted. It was a long time since the hotel owner had been referred to as an "important man."

Then he went with the same talk to five others—the blacksmith, the carpenter and odd-jobber, the storekeeper, and two men whom he had marked when he first halted near the hotel veranda. To his invitation each of them gave a quick assent. There had been something mysterious in the manner in which this timid-eyed giant had descended upon the town from nowhere, and now they felt that they were about to come to the heart of the reason of his visit.

The invitation to the sheriff was delivered by the proprietor of the hotel, and he said just enough—and no more—to bring the sheriff straight to the hotel. Anderson arrived with his best pair of guns in his holsters, for the sheriff was a two-gun man of the best variety. He came with the aggressive manner of one ready to beat down all opposition, but when he stepped into the room, his manner changed. For he found sitting about the table in the dining room, which was to be the scene of the conference, the six most influential men of the town—men strong enough to reelect him next year, or to throw him permanently out of office.

At the lower end of the table stood Bull Hunter, his arms folded, his face blank. Standing with the light from the lamp shining upon his face, the others seated, he seemed a man among pygmies.

"Shall I lock the door?" asked the proprietor, and he turned to Bull, as if the later had the right to dictate.

Bull nodded.

"All right, sheriff," the proprietor went on to

explain. "Our young friend yonder says that he's got something to say to you. He's asked each of us to hang around and be a witness. Are you ready?"

"Jud," burst out the sheriff, "you're an idiot! This overgrown booby needs a horsewhipping, and that's the sort of an answer I'd like to make to him."

Having delivered this broadside, he strode up and confronted Bull. It was a very poor move. In the first place, the sheriff had insulted one of the men who was about to act as his official judge. In the second place, by putting himself so close to Bull, he made himself appear a trifle ludicrous. Also, if he expected to throw Bull out of poise with this blustering, he failed. It was not that Bull did not feel fear, but he had seen a curious thing—the sinewy, long neck of the sheriff, and he was wondering what would happen if one of his hands should grip that throat—for a single instant. He grew so fascinated by this study that he forgot his fear of the sheriff's guns.

Anderson hastened to retreat from his false position. "Gents," he said, "excuse me for getting edgy. But, if you want me to listen to this fellow's talk—"

"Hunter is his name—Bull Hunter," said the proprietor.

The sheriff took his place at the far end of the

long table. Like Bull, he preferred to stand. "Start in your talk," he commanded.

"It looks to me," said Bull gently, "that they's only one gent here that's wearing a gun." He had thrown his own belt on a chair; and now he fixed his eyes on the weapons of Anderson.

The sheriff glared. "You want me to take off my guns? Son, I'd rather go naked!"

Jud, the hotel man, had already been insulted once by the sheriff, and he had been biding his time. This seemed an excellent opening. "Looks to me," he remarked, "like Mr. Hunter was right. He's got something pretty serious to say, and he don't want to take no chances on you cutting him short with a bullet!"

The sheriff glared at Bull and then cast a swift glance over the faces of the others. He read upon them only one expression—a cold curiosity. Plainly they agreed with Jud, and the sheriff gave way. He took off his belt and tossed it upon a chair near him. Then he faced Bull again, but he faced the big man with half his confidence destroyed. As he had said, he felt worse than naked without his revolvers under his touch, but now he attempted to brave out the situation.

"Well," he said jocularly, "what you going to accuse me of, Bull Hunter?"

"I'm just going to tell a little story that I been thinking about," said Bull.

"Story—nothing!" exclaimed Anderson.

"Wait a minute," broke in Jud. "Let him tell this his own way—I think you'd best, sheriff!"

Bull was looking at the sheriff and through him into the distance. After all, it was a story, as distinctly a story as if he had it in a book. As he began to tell it, he forgot Sheriff Anderson at the farther end of the table. He talked slowly, bringing the words out one by one, as if what he said were coming to him by inspiration—a kind of second sight.

"It starts in," said Bull, "the other night when the gent come in with word that Pete Reeve was out playing cards with Armstrong and losing money. When the sheriff heard that, he started to thinking. He was remembering how he'd hated Armstrong for a good many years, and that made him think that maybe Armstrong would get into trouble with Reeve, because Reeve is a pretty good shot, and the sheriff hoped that, if it come to a showdown, Reeve would shoot Armstrong full of holes. And that started him wishing pretty strong that Armstrong would get killed!"

"Do I have to stand here and listen to this fool talk?" demanded the sheriff.

"I'm just supposing," said Bull. "Surely they ain't any harm in just supposing?"

"Not a bit," decided Jud, who had taken the position of main arbiter.

"Well, the sheriff got to wishing Armstrong was dead so strong that it didn't seem he could stand to have him living much more. He told the folks that he was going out to see that no harm come to Armstrong from Reeve. Then he got on his hoss and went out. All the way he was thinking hard. Armstrong was the gent that was sheriff before Anderson; Armstrong was the gent that might get the job and throw him out again. Ain't that clear? Well, the sheriff gets close to the cabin and—"

He paused and slowly extended his long arm toward the sheriff. "What'd you do then?"

"Me? I heard a shot—"

"You left your hoss standing in the brush near the house," interrupted Bull, "and you went along on foot."

"Does that sound reasonable, a gent going on foot when he might ride?" demanded the sheriff.

"You didn't want to make no noise," said Bull, and his great voice swallowed the protest of the sheriff.

Anderson cast another glance at the listeners. Plainly they were fascinated by this tale, and they were following it step by step with nods.

"You didn't make no noise, either," went on Bull Hunter. "You slipped up to the cabin real soft, and you climbed up on the east side of the house over some rocks."

"Why in reason should a man climb over rocks? Why wouldn't he go right to the door?"

"Because you didn't want to be seen."

"Then why not the west window, fool!"

"You tried that window first, but they was some dry brush lying in front of it, and you couldn't come close enough to look in without making a noise stepping on the dead wood. So then you went around to the other side and climbed over the rocks until you could look into the cabin. Am I right?"

"I—no, curse you, no! Of course you ain't right!" shouted Anderson.

"Looking right through that window," said Bull heavily, "you seen Armstrong, the man you hated, facing you, and, with his back turned, was Pete Reeve. You said to yourself: 'Drop Armstrong with a bullet, catch Reeve, and put the blame on him!' Then you pulled your gun."

He pushed aside the ponderous armchair which stood beside him at the head of the table.

"Say," shouted the sheriff, paler than ever now, "what are you accusing me of?"

"Murder!" thundered Bull Hunter.

The roar of Bull's voice chained every one in his place, the sheriff with staring eyes, and Jud in the act of raising his hand.

"I'll jail you for slander!" said the sheriff, fighting to assurance and knowing that he was betrayed by his pallor and by the icy perspiration which he felt on his forehead.

"Anderson," said Bull, "I seen the marks of them iron heels of yours on the rock!"

That was a little thing, of course. As evidence it would not have convinced the most prejudiced jury in the world, but Sheriff Anderson was not weighting small points. Into his mind leaped one image—the whiteness of those rocks on which he had stood and the indelible mark his heels must have made against that whiteness. He was lost, he felt, and he acted on the impulse to fight for his life.

One last glance he cast at the six listeners, and in their wide-eyed interest he read his own damnation. Then Anderson whirled and leaped for his belt with the guns.

Out of six throats came six yells of fear; there was a noise of chairs being pushed back and a wild scramble to find safety under the table. Jud, risking a moment's delay, knocked the chimney off the lamp before he dived. The flame leaped once and went out, but the pale moonshine poured through the window and filled the room with a weird play of shadows.

What Bull Hunter saw was not the escape of the sheriff, but a sudden blind rage against everything and everybody. It was a passion that set him trembling through all of his great body. One touch of trust, one word of encouragement had been enough to make him a giant to tear up the stump in the presence of Jessie and his cousins; how far more mighty he was in the grip of this new emotion, this rage.

His own gun was far away, but guns were not what he wanted. They were uncongenial toys to his great hands. Instead, he reached down and caught up that massive chair of oak, built to resist time, built to bear even such a bulk as that of Bull Hunter with ease. Yet he caught it up in one hand, weighed it behind his head at the full limit of his extended arm, and then, bending forward, he catapulted the great missile down the length of the table. It hit the lamp on the way and splintered it to small bits, its momentum unimpeded. Hurtling on across the table it shot at the sheriff as he whirled with his guns in his hands.

Fast as the chair shot forward, the hand of the sheriff was faster still. Bull saw the big guns twitch up, silver in the moonshine. They exploded in one voice, as if the flying mass of wood were an animate object. Then the sheriff was struck and hurled crashing along the floor.

Chapter Nine

On the Marsh

At that fall the six men scampered from beneath the table to seize the downed man. There was no need of their haste. Sheriff Anderson was a wreck rather than a fighting man. One arm was horribly crumpled beneath him; his ribs were shattered; there was a great gash where the rung of the chair had cut into the bone like a knife.

They stood chattering about the fallen man, straightening him out, feeling his pulse, making sure that he, who would soon hang at the will of the law, was alive. Outside, voices were rushing toward them, doors slamming.

Bull Hunter broke through the circle, bent over the limp body, and drew a big bundle of keys from a pocket. Then, without a word, he went back to the far end of the room, buckled on his gun belt, and in silence left the room.

The others paid no heed. They and the new-comers, who had poured into the room, were fascinated by the work of the giant rather than the giant's self. They had a lantern, swinging dull light and grotesque shadows across the place now, and by the illumination, two of the men went to the wall and picked up the great oaken chair. They raised it slowly between them, a battered mass of disconnected wood. Then they looked to the far end of the long table where he, who had thrown the missile, had stood. Another line had been written into the history of Bull Hunter—the first line that was written in red.

Bull himself was on his way to the jail. He found it unguarded. The deputy had gone to find the cause of the commotion at the hotel. The steel bars, moreover, were sufficient to re-tain the prisoner and keep out would-be res-cuers.

In the dim light of his lantern, Bull saw that Pete Reeve was sitting cross-legged on his bunk, like a little, dried-up idol, smoking a cigarette. His only greeting to the big man was a lifting of the eyebrows. But, when the big key was fitted into the lock and the lock turned, he showed his first signs of interest. He was standing up when Bull opened the door and strode in.

"Have you got your things?" said Bull curtly.

"What things, big fellow?"

"Why, guns and things—and your hat, of course."

Pete Reeve walked to the corner of the cell and took a sombrero off the wall. "Here's the hat," he answered, "but they ain't passing out guns to jailbirds—not in these parts!"

"You ain't a jailbird," answered Bull, "so we'll get that gun. Know where it is?"

Reeve followed without a question through the open door, only stopping as he passed beyond the bars, to look back to them with a shudder. It was the first sign of emotion he had shown since his arrest. But his step was lighter and quicker as he followed Bull into the front room.

"In that closet, yonder," said Reeve, pointing to a door. "That's where they keep the guns."

Bull shook out his bundle of keys into the great palm of his hand.

"Not those keys—the deputy has the key to the closet," said Pete. "I saw Anderson give it to him."

Bull sighed. "I ain't got much time, partner," he said. Approaching the door, he examined it wistfully. "But, maybe, they's another way." He drew back a little, raised his right leg, and smashed the heavy cowhide boot against the door. The wood split from top to bottom, and Bull's leg was driven on through the aperture. He paused to wrench the fragments of the door from lock and hinges and then beckoned to Pete Reeve. "Look for your gun in here, Reeve."

The little man cast one twinkling glance at his companion and then was instantly among the litter of the closet floor. He emerged strapping a belt about him, the holster tugging far down, so that the muzzle of the gun was almost at his knee. Bull appreciated the diminutive size of the man for the first time, seeing him in conjunction with the big gun on his thigh.

There was an odd change in the little man also, the moment his gun was in place. He tugged his broad-brimmed hat a little lower across his eyes and poised himself, as if on tiptoe; his glance was a constant flicker about the room until it came to rest on Bull. "Suppose you lemme in on the meaning of all this. Who are you and where do you figure on letting me loose? What in thunder is it all about?"

"We'll talk later. Now you got to get started."

Bull waved to the door. Pete Reeve darted past him with noiseless steps and paused a moment at the threshold of the jail. Plainly he was ready for fight or flight, and his right hand was toying constantly with the holstered butt of his gun. Bull followed to the outside.

"Hosses?" asked the little man curtly.

"On foot," answered Bull with equal brevity, and he led the way straight across the street. There was no danger of being seen. All the life of the town was drawn to a center about the hotel. Lights were flashing behind its windows, men were constantly pounding across the veranda, running in and out. Bull led the way past the building and cut for the cottonwoods.

"And now?" demanded Pete Reeve. "Now, partner?"

That word stung Bull. It had not been applied to him more than half a dozen times in his life, together with its implications of free and equal brotherhood. To be called partner by the great man who had conquered terrible Uncle Bill Campbell!

"They's a mess in the hotel," said Bull, explaining as shortly as he could. "Seems that Sheriff Anderson was the gent that done the killing of Armstrong. It got found out and the sheriff tried to get away. Lots of noise and trouble."

"Ah," said Reeve, "it was him, then—the old hound! I might of knowed! But I kep' on figuring that they was two of 'em! Well, the sheriff was a handy boy with his gun. Did he drop anybody before they got him? I heard two guns go off like one. Them must of been the sheriff's cannons."

"They was," said Bull, "but them bullets didn't hit nothing but wood."

"Wild, eh? Shot into the wall?"

"Nope. Into a chair."

The little man was struggling and panting and sometimes breaking into a trot to keep up with the immense strides of his companion. "A chair? You don't say so!"

Bull was silent.

"How come he shot at a chair? Drunk?"

"The chair was sailing through the air at him."

"H'm!" returned Pete Reeve. "Somebody threwed a chair at him, and the sheriff got rattled and shot at it instead of dodging? Well, I've seen a pile of funnier things than that happen in gun play, off and on. Who threw the chair?"

"I did."

"You?" He squinted up at the lofty form of Bull Hunter. "What name did you say?" he asked gently.

"Hunter is my name. Mostly they call me Bull."

"You got the size for that name, partner. So you cleaned up the sheriff with a chair?" He sighed. "I wished I'd been there to see it. But who got the inside on the sheriff?"

"I dunno what you mean?"

Pete Reeve looked closely at his companion. Plainly he was bewildered, somewhere between a smile and a frown.

"I mean who found out that the sheriff done it?"

"He told it himself," said Bull.

"Drunk, eh?"

"Nope. Not drunk. He was asked if he didn't do the murder."

"Great guns! Who asked him?"

"I done it," said Bill as simply as ever.

Reeve bit his lip. He had just put Bull down as a simple-minded hulk. He was forced to revise his opinion.

"You done that? You follered him up, eh?"

"I just done a little thinking. So I asked him."

Reeve shook his head. "Maybe you hypnotized him," he suggested.

"Nope. I just asked him. I got a lot of folks sitting around, and then I begun telling the sheriff how he done the shooting."

"And he admitted it?"

"Nope. He jumped for a gun."

"And then you heaved a chair at him." Pete Reeve drew in a long breath. "But what reason did you have, son? I got to ask you that before I thank you the way I want to thank you. But, before you kick out, you'll find that Pete Reeve is as a friend."

"My reason was," said Bull, "that I had business to do with you that couldn't be done in a jail. So I had to get you out."

"And now where're we headed?"

"Where we can do that business."

They had reached a broad break in the cottonwoods; the moonlight was falling softly and brightly.

Bull paused and looked around him. "I guess this'll have to do," he declared.

"All right, son. You can be as mysterious as you want. Now what you got me here for?"

"To kill you," said Bull gently.

Pete Reeve flinched back. Then he tapped his holster, made sure of the gun, became more easy. "That's interesting," he announced. "You couldn't wait for the law to hang me, eh?"

Bull began explaining laboriously. He pushed back his hat and began to count off his points into the palm of one hand. "You shot up Uncle Bill Campbell," he explained. "It ain't that I got any grudge agin' you for that, but you see, Uncle Bill took me in young and give me a home all these years. I thought it would sort of pay him back if I run you down. So I walked across the mountains and come after you."

"Wait!" exclaimed Pete Reeve. "You walked?"

"Yep," he went on, heedless of the fact that Pete Reeve was peering earnestly into the face of his companion, now puckered with the earnest frown of thought. "I come down hoping to get you and kill you. Besides, that wouldn't only pay back Uncle Bill. It would make him think I was a man. You see, Reeve, I ain't quick thinking, and I ain't bright. I ain't got a quick tongue and sharp eyes, and they been treating me like I was a kid all my life. So I got to do something. I got to! I ain't got anything agin' you, but you just happen to be the one that I got to fight. Stand over yonder by that stump. I'll stand here, and we'll fight fair and square."

Pete Reeve obeyed, his movements slow, as if they were the result of hypnotism. "Bull," he said rather faintly, looking at the towering bulk of his opponent, "I dunno. Maybe I'm going nutty. But I figure that you come down here to kill me for the sake of getting your uncle to pat you on the back once or twice. And you find you can't get at me because I'm in jail, so you work out a murder mystery to get me out, and then you tackle me. You say you ain't very bright. I dunno. Maybe you ain't bright, but you're mighty different!"

He paused and rubbed his forehead. "Son, I've seen pretty good men in my day, but I ain't never seen one that I cotton to like I do to you. You've saved my life. How can you figure on me going out and taking yours, now?"

"You ain't going to, maybe," said Bull calmly. "Maybe I'll get to you."

"Son," answered the other almost sadly, shaking his head, "when I'm right, with a good, steady nerve, they ain't any man in the world that can sling a gun with me. And tonight I'm right. If it comes to a showdown—but are you pretty good with a gun yourself, Bull?"

"No," answered Bull frankly. "I ain't any good compared to an expert like you. But I'm good enough to take a chance."

"Them sort of chances ain't taken twice, Bull!"

"You see," said Bull, "I'm going to make a rush as I pull the gun, and if I get to you before I'm dead, well—all I ask is to lay my hands on you, you see?"

The little man shuddered and blinked. "I see," he said, and swallowed with difficulty. "But, in the name of reason, Bull, have sense! Lemme talk! I'll tell you what that uncle of yours was—"

"Don't talk!" exclaimed Bull Hunter. "I sort of like you, partner, and it sort of breaks me down to hear you talk. Don't talk, but listen. The next time that frog croaks we go for our guns, eh? That frog off in the marsh!"

He had hardly spoken before the ominous sound was heard, and Bull reached for his gun. For all his bulk of hand and unwieldy arms, the gun came smoothly, swiftly into his hand. He would have had an ordinary man covered, long before the latter had his gun muzzle clear of the leather. But Pete Reeve was no ordinary man. His arm jerked down; his fingers flickered down and up. They went down empty; they came up with the burden of a long revolver, shining in the moonlight, and he fired before Bull's gun came to the level for a shot.

Only Pete Reeve knew the marvel of his own shooting this day. He had sworn a solemn and silent oath that he would not kill this faithful, courageous fellow from the mountains. He could have planted a bullet where the life lay, at any instant of the fight. But he fired for another purpose. The moment Bull reached for his weapon he had lurched forward, aiming to shoot as he ran. Pete Reeve set himself a double goal. His first intention was to disarm the giant; the other was to stop his rush. For, once within the grip of those big fingers, his life would be squeezed out like the juice from an orange.

His task was doubly difficult in the moonlight. But the first shot went home nicely, aimed as exactly as a scientist finds a spot with his instruments. Where the moon's rays splashed across the bare right forearm of Bull, he sent a bullet that slashed through the great muscles. The revolver dropped from the nerveless hand of the giant, but Bull never paused. On he came, empty-handed, but with power of death, as the little man well knew, in the fingers of his extended left hand. He came with a snarl, a savage intake of breath, as he felt the hot slash of Pete's bullet. But Reeve, standing erect like some duelist of old, his left hand tucked into the hollow of his back, took the great gambling chance and refused to shoot to kill.

He placed his second shot more effectively, for this time he must stop that tremendous body, advancing upon him. He found one critical spot. Between the knee and the thigh, halfway up on the inside of the left leg, he drove that second bullet with the precision of a surgeon. The leg crumpled under Bull and sent him pitching forward on his face.

Perhaps the marsh ground was unstable, but it seemed to Pete Reeve that the very earth quaked beneath his feet as the big man fell. He swung his gun wide and leaned to see how serious was the damage he had done. Bleeding would be the great danger.

But that fraction of a second brought him into another peril. The giant heaved up on his sound right leg and his sound left arm, and flung himself forward, two limbs dangling uselessly. With a hideously contorted face, Bull swung his left arm in a wide circle for a grip and scooped in Pete Reeve, as the latter sprang back with a cry of horror.

The action swept Pete in and crushed his gun hand and arm against the body of his assailant, paralyzing his only power of attack or defense.

Reeve was carried down to the ground as if beneath the bulk of a mountain. There was no question of sparing life now. Pete Reeve began to fight for life. He wrested at his gun to tug it free, but found it anchored. He pulled the trigger, and the gun spoke loud and clear, but the bullet plunged into empty space. Then he felt that left arm begin to move, and the hand worked up behind his back like a great spider.

Higher it rose, and the huge, thick fingers reached up and around his throat, fumbling to get at the windpipe. Pete Reeve made his last effort; it was like striving to free himself from a ton's weight. Hysteria of fear and horror seized him, and his voice gave utterance to his terror. As he screamed, the big fingers joined around his throat. Any further pressure would end him!

He looked up into the glaring eyes and the contorted face of the giant; the rasping, panting breath paralyzed his senses. There was a slight inward contraction of the grip; then it ceased.

Miraculously he felt the great hand relax and fall away. The bulk was heaved away from him, and staggering to his own feet, he saw Bull Hunter supported against a tree, one leg useless, one arm streaming.

"I couldn't seem to do it," said Bull Hunter thickly. "I couldn't noways seem to do it, Reeve. You see, I sort of like you, and I couldn't kill you, Pete."

When Pete Reeve recovered from his astonishment he said: "You can do more. You can go home and tell that infernal hound of an uncle of yours that you had the life of Pete Reeve under your finger tips and that you didn't take it. It's the second time I've owed my life, and both times in one day, and both times to one man. You tell your uncle that!"

The big man sagged still more against the tree. "I'll never go home, Pete, unless ghosts walk; and I'll never tell Uncle Bill anything, unless the ghosts talk. I'm dying pretty pronto, I think, Pete."

"Dyin'? You ain't hurt bad, Bull!"

"It's the bleeding; all the senses is running out of my head—like water—and the moon—is turning black—and—" He slumped down at the foot of the tree.

Chapter Ten

Bullets with Sense

When old Farmer Morton and his son came in their buckboard through the marshes, they heard the screaming of Pete Reeve for help. Leaving their team, they bolted across country to the open glade. There they found Pete still shouting for help, kneeling above the body of a man, and working desperately to arrange an effectual tourniquet. They ran close and discovered the two men.

Old Morton knew enough rude surgery to stop the bleeding. It was he who counted the pulse and listened to the heart. "Low," he said, "very low—life is just flickerin', stranger."

"If they's as much light of life in him," said Pete Reeve, "as the flicker of a candle, I'll fan it up till it's as big as a forest fire. Man, he's got to live."

"H'm!" said Morton. "And how come the shooting?"

"Stop your fool questions," said Reeve. "Help me get him to town and to a bed."

It was useless to attempt to carry that great, loose-limbed body. They brought the buckboard perilously through the shrubbery and then managed, with infinite labor, to lift Bull Hunter into it. With Pete Reeve supporting the head of the wounded man and cautioning them to drive gently, they managed the journey to the town as softly as possible. At the hotel a strongarmed cortege bore Bull to a bed, and they carried him reverently. Had his senses been with him he would have wondered greatly; and had his uncle, or his uncle's sons, been there, they would surely have laughed uproariously.

In the hotel room Pete Reeve took command at once. "He's too big to die," he told the dubious doctor. "He's got to live. And the minute you say he can't, out you go and another doc comes in. Now do your work."

The doctor, haunted by the deep, fiery eyes of the gunfighter, stepped into the room to minister to his patient. He had a vague feeling that, if Bull Hunter died, Pete Reeve would blame him for lack of care. In truth, Pete seemed ready to blame every one. He threatened to destroy the whole village if a dog was allowed to howl in the night, or if the baby next door were permitted to cry in the day.

Silence settled over the little town—silence and the fear of Pete Reeve. Pete himself never left the sick room. Wide-eyed, silent-footed, he was ever about. He seemed never to sleep, and the doctor swore that the only reason Bull Hunter did not die was because death feared to enter the room while the awful Reeve was there.

But the long hours of unconsciousness and delirium wore away. Then came the critical period when a relapse was feared. Finally the time came when it could be confidently stated that Bull was recovering his health and his strength.

All this filled a matter of weeks. Bull was still unable to leave his bed. He was dull and listless, bony of hand, and liable to sleep many hours through the very heart of the day. At this point of his recovery the door opened one day, and, in the warmth of the afternoon, a big man came into the room, shutting the door softly behind him.

Bull turned his head slowly and then blinked, for it was the unshaven face of his cousin, Harry Campbell, that he saw. With his eyes closed, Bull wondered why that face was so distinctly unpleasant. When he opened them again, Harry had drawn closer, his hat pushed on the back of his head, after the manner of a baffled man, and a faint smile working at the corners of his lips. He took the limp hand of Bull in his and squeezed it cautiously. Then he laid the hand back on the sheet and grinned more confidently at Bull.

"Well, I'll be hanged, Bull, here you are as big as life, pretty near, and you don't act like you knew me!"

"Sure I do. Sit down, Harry. What brung you all this ways?"

"Why, anxious to see how you was doing."

Again Bull blinked. Such anxiety from Harry was a mystery.

"They ain't talking about much else up our way," said Harry, "but how you come across the mountains in the storm, and how big you are, and how you got the sheriff, and how you rushed Pete Reeve bare-handed. Sure is some story! All the way down I just had to say that I was Bull Hunter's cousin, to get free meals!" He licked his lips and grinned again. "So I come down to see how you was."

"I'm doing tolerable fair," said Bull slowly, "and it was good of you to come this long ways to ask that question. How's things to home?"

"Dad's bunged up for life; can't do nothing but cuss, but at that he lays over anything you ever hear." Harry's eyes flicked nervously about the room. "It was him that sent me down! Where's Reeve?"

This was in a whisper. Bull gestured toward the next room.

"Asleep? Can he hear if I talk?"

"Asleep," said Bull. "Been up with me two days. I took a bad turn a while back. Pete's helping himself to a nap, and he needs one!"

"Now, listen!" said Harry. "Dad figured this out, and dad's mostly never wrong. He says: 'Reeve shot up Bull. Now he's hanging around trying to make up by nursing Bull, according to reports, because he's afraid of what Bull'll do when he gets back on his feet. But Bull has got to know that, even when he's back on his feet, he can't beat Reeve—not while Reeve can pull a gun. Nobody can beat that devil. If he wants to beat Reeve, just take advantage of him while Reeve ain't expecting anything—which means while Bull is sick.' Do you get what dad means?"

"Sort of," said Bull faintly. He shut out the eager, dirty, unshaven face. "I'll just close my eyes against the light. I can hear you pretty well. Go on."

"Here's the idea. Everybody knows you hate Reeve, and Reeve fears you. Otherwise would he act like this, aside from being afraid of a lynching, in case you should die? No, he wouldn't. Well, one of these days you take this gun"—here Harry shoved one under the pillow of Bull—"and call Pete Reeve over to you, and when he leans over your bed, blow his brains out! That's easy, and it'll do what you'll want to do some day. You hear? Then you can say that Reeve started something—that you shot in self-defense. Everybody'll believe you, and you'll get one big name for killing Reeve! You foller me?"

Bull opened his eyes, but they were squinting as though he was in the severest pain. "Listen, Harry," he said at last. "I been thinking things out. I owe a lot to your dad for taking me in and keeping me. But all I owe him I can pay back in cash—some day. I don't owe him no love. Nor you, neither."

Harry had risen to his feet with a snarl.

"Sit down," said Bull, letting his great voice swell ever so little. "I'm pretty near dead, but I'm still man enough to wring the neck of a skunk! Sit down!"

Harry obeyed limply, and his giant cousin went on, his voice softening again. "When you come in I closed my eyes," said Bull, "because it seemed to me like you was a dream. I'd been awake. I'd been living among men that sort of liked me and respected me and didn't laugh at me. And then you come, and I saw your dirty face, and it made me think of a bad nightmare I'd had when you and your brother and your dad treated me worse'n a dog. Well, Harry, I'm through with that dream. I'll never go back to it. I'm going to stay awake the rest of my life. It was your dad that put the wish to kill Reeve into my head with his talk. I met Reeve, and Reeve pumped some bullets with sense into me. He let out some of my life, but he let in a lot of knowledge. Among other things he showed me what a friend might be. He's stayed here and nursed me and talked to me—like I was his equal, almost, instead of being sort of simple, like I really am. And I've made up my mind that I'm going to cut loose from remembering you folks in the mountains. I ain't your kind. I don't want to be your kind. I want to fight, like Pete Reeve. I don't want to murder like a Campbell! All the way through, I want to be like Pete Reeve. He don't know it. Maybe when I'm well he'll go off by himself. But whether he's near or far, I've adopted him. I'm going to pattern after him, and the happiest day of my life will be when I earn the right to have this man, that I tried to kill, come and take my hand and call me 'friend!' I guess that answers you, Harry. Now get out and take my talk back to your dad, and don't trouble me no more—you spoil my sleep!"

As he spoke the door of the next room opened softly. Pete Reeve stood at the entrance. Harry, shaking with fear, backed toward the other door, then leaped far out, and whirled out of sight with a slam and clatter of feet on the stair. Pete Reeve came slowly to the bedside.

"I was awake, son," he said, "and I couldn't help hearing.

Bull flushed heavily.

"It's the best thing I ever heard," said Pete. "The best thing that's ever come to my ears—partner!"

With that word their hands joined. In reality, far more than he dreamed, Bull had been born again.

Chapter Eleven

Gun Practice

When they were together, they made a study in contrasts. By seeing one it was possible to imagine the other. For instance, seeing the high, narrow forehead, peaked face, the gray-flecked hair of Pete Reeve, his nervous step, his piercing and uneasy eye—seeing this man with his body from which all spare flesh was wasted so that he remained only muscle and nerve, it was easy to conjure up the figure of Bull Hunter by thinking of opposites.

Their very voices held a world of difference. The tone of Pete Reeve was pitched a little high, hard, and somewhat nasal, and when he was angry his words came shrill and ringing. The mere sound of his voice was irritating—it put one on edge with expectancy of action. Whereas the full, deep, slow, musical voice of Bull Hunter was a veritable sleep producer. Men might fear Charlie Bull Hunter because of his tremendous bulk; but children, hearing his voice, were unafraid.

The motions of Pete Reeve were as fast and as deft as the whiplash striking of a snake. The motions of Bull Hunter were premeditated and cautious, as befitted one whose hands might crush what they touched, and whose footfall made a flooring groan.

He sat cross-legged on the floor, his back against the wall. They had moved a ponderous stool into the room so that Bull might have something on which to sit, but long habit had made him uneasy in a chair, and he kept to the floor by preference, with the great square chin resting on his fist and his knee supporting his elbow. That position pressed the forearm against the biceps and the big muscles bulged out on either side, vast as the thigh of a strong man.

With lionlike wrinkles of attention between his eyes, he listened to the exposition of the little man, and followed his movements with patient submission—like a pupil to whom a great master has consented to unfold the secrets of his brush work; in such a manner did Bull Hunter drink in the words and the acts of Pete Reeve. And, indeed, where guns were the subject of conversation it would have been hard to find a man more thoroughly equipped to pose as an expert than Pete Reeve. That fleshless hand, all speed of motion as it whipped out the gun from the nerve and sinew, became an incredible ghost with the holster, and the long, heavy Colt danced and flashed at his finger tips as though it were a gilded shadow.

As he worked he talked, and as he talked he strode constantly back and forth through the room with his light-falling, mincing steps. He grew excited. He flushed. There came a thrill and a ring and a deepening of the voice. For the master was indeed talking of the secrets of his craft.

A thousand men of the mountains and the cattle ranges, men who, for personal pride or for physical need, studied accuracy and speed in gun play, would have paid untold prices to learn these secrets from the lips of the little man. To Bull Hunter the mysteries were revealed for nothing, freely, and drilled and drummed into him through the weeks of his convalescence; and still the lessons continued now that he was hale and hearty once more— as the cleanswept platters from which he ate three times a day gave evidence.

"I've practiced, you admit," said Bull in his slow voice, as Pete Reeve came to a pause. "But I haven't got your way with a gun, Pete. You've got a genius for it. I don't blame you for laughing at me when I try to get out my gun fast. I can shoot straight. That's because I haven't any nerves, as you say, but I'll never be able to get out a gun as fast as a thought—the way you do. Fact is, Pete, I don't think fast, you know."

"Shut up!" exploded Pete Reeve, who had been inwardly chafing with impatience during the whole length of this speech. "Sometimes you talk like a fool, Bull, and this is one time!"

Bull shook his head. "My arms are too big," he said sadly. "The muscle gets in my way. I can feel it bind when I try to jerk out the gun fast. Better give up the job, Pete. I sure appreciate all the pains you've taken with me—but I'll never be a gunfighter."

Pete Reeve shook his head with a sigh and then dropped into a chair, growing suddenly inert.

"No use," he groaned. "All because you ain't got any confidence, Bull." He leaned forward in his sudden way. "Know something? I been keeping it back, but now I'll tell you the straight of it. You're faster with a gun right now than four men out of five!"

Bull gaped in amazement.

"Fact!" cried Reeve. "You get it out slicker

than most; and after it's out, you shoot as straight as any man I've ever seen. Trouble is, you don't appreciate yourself. You've had it drilled into you so long that you're stupid that now you believe it. All nonsense! You got more than a million have and you're fast right now on the draw. Once get hold of how important it is, and you'll keep trying. But you think it's only a game. You just play at it; you don't work! I wish you could have seen me when I was first practicing with a gun! I lived with it. Hours every day it was my companion, and right up to now, there ain't a day goes by that I don't spend some time keeping on edge with my revolver. Bull, you'll have to do the same thing. You hear?"

He sprang up again. It was impossible for him to remain seated a long time.

"You think it don't mean much. Look here!"

The Colt flicked into his hand and lay trembling in his palm, and as he talked, it shifted smoothly, as if of its own volition, forward toward his finger tips, backward, to the side, dropping out until it seemed about to fall, only to be caught with one finger through the trigger-guard and spun up again. Always the heavy weapon was in motion as though some of the nervous spirit of Reeve had entered the heavy metal. It responded to his thoughts rather than to his muscles. Bull Hunter gazed enchanted.

He was accustomed to forgetting himself and admiring others.

"Look here!" went on the little man. "Look at me. I weigh about a hundred and twenty. I'm skinny. I'm a runt. And look at you. You weigh—Heaven knows what!—no fat, but all muscle. All muscle from your head to your feet. You're the strongest man that I ever seen. Take me, I'm not a coward; but you, Bull, you don't know what fear means. Well, there you are, without fear, and stronger than three strong men. You're pretty fast with a gun, and you shoot straight as a hawk looks. And still, if we stood face to face and went for our guns, I'd live; and you with all your muscle would be dead, Bull."

"I know," Bull nodded.

"That's what this gun means," cried Pete. "This gun, and the fact that I can get it out of the leather faster'n you do. Not very much faster. But by just as much quicker as it takes for an eyelid to wink. That ain't much time, but it's enough time to mean life or death! That's all! I'm not the only man that's faster'n you are. They's others. I've never been beat to the draw, but they's some that's shot so close to me that it sounded like one gun going off—with a sort of a stammer. And any one of those men would of shot you dead, Bull, if you'd fought 'em. Now, knowing that, tell me are you going to keep practicing?"

"I'll keep tryin, Pete. But I'll never get much faster. You see—my arm—it's too big—too heavy. It gets in my way, handling a little thing like a revolver!"

Pete spun the big Colt and shoved it back into the holster so incredibly fast that the steel hissed against the leather.

"There you go running yourself down," he muttered.

He began to pace the room again, biting his nether lip, and now and then shooting side glances at Bull, glances partly guilty and partly scornful. Presently he came to a halt. He had also come to a new resolution, one that cost him so much that beads of perspiration came out on his forehead.

"Bull," he said gravely, "I'm going to tell you the secret."

"You've told me a dozen already," Bull sighed. "You've taught me how to swing the muzzle up, and not too far up, and how to lean back instead of forward, and how to harden the arm muscles just as I pull the trigger, and how to squeeze with the whole hand and keep my wrist stiff, and how—"

"None of them things counts," said Pete gravely, almost sadly, "compared to what I'm going to tell you. Stand up!"

It was plain that he was going to give something from the deeps of his mind. The cost and importance of it made his eyes like steel and drew his mouth to a thin, straight line.

Bull Hunter arose; and as the great body unfolded and the legs straightened, it seemed that he would never reach his full height. At length he stood, enormous, wide, towering. He was not a freak, but simply a perfectly proportioned man increased to a huge scale.

Pete Reeve canted his head back and looked into the face of the giant. There was a momentary affectionate appreciation in his eye. Then he hardened his expression.

"Let your arm hang loose."

Bull Hunter obeyed. The hand came just above the holster that was strapped on his thigh. All these weeks Pete Reeve had kept him from going an instant without that gun except when he slept. And even when he slept the gun had to be under his pillow.

"Because it helps to have it near all the time," Pete had explained. "It sort of soaks into your dreams. It's never out of your mind. It haunts you, like the face of the girl you love. You see!"

Bull Hunter did not see, but he had nodded humbly, after his fashion, and obeyed. Now, with his arm fallen loose at his side he peered studiously into the face of his master gunman and waited for the next order.

135

"Draw!"

The command was snapped out; Bull's gun whipped from the holster; and Pete Reeve drew in the same instant, carelessly, his eyes watching the movement of Bull instead of paying heed to his own weapon. Then he shook his head and put his gun up again, but Bull followed the example almost reluctantly.

"Nearly beat you that time, Pete," he exclaimed happily. "But maybe you weren't half trying?"

"Beat me?" sneered Pete. "I wasn't half trying, but you didn't beat me. I shot you twice before you had your muzzle in line. I shot you in the throat and through the teeth before your gun was ready."

Bull, with a shrug of the massive shoulders, touched the mentioned places and looked with awe at the little man.

"Now, listen!"

Bull grew tense.

"Watch my draw!"

Pete did not put his hand near the butt of his weapon. He held his arm out before him, dangling in the air. There was a convulsive movement. One could see the imaginary weapon shoot from the holster and become level and rigid, pointed at its mark.

"I've seen before—fast as my eye could go," Bull sighed.

136

"Look again," said Pete, gritting his teeth with impatience. "This time I'm going so slow a cow could see and beat me."

He made the same motion, but to an ordinary eye it was still as fast as light. Bull shook his head.

"Idiot!" cried Pete, his voice jumping up the scale, flat and harsh and piercing. "It's the wrist! Not the arm, but the—"

He stopped with an expression of dismay. Even now he regretted revealing the mystery, it seemed. But then he went on.

"I found out quick that I couldn't beat a good gunman if I used the old methods. Practice makes perfect; they practiced as much as I did. So I studied the methods and the great idea come to me. They all use the whole arm. Look at you! Your shoulder bulges up when you make the draw, and you raise the whole arm. Matter of fact, you'd ought only to use your fingers. Not stir a muscle above the wrist. Now try!"

Bull tried—the gun did not come clear of the holster.

"No good," he said gravely. "It's magic when you do it, Pete. It just makes a fool of me."

"Shut up and listen!" Pete said sharply. "I'm telling you a thing that'll save your life some day!"

He drew a little closer. His emotion made him

137

swell to a greater stature, and he rose a little on tiptoe as if partly to make up for the differences between their bulks.

Bull obeyed.

"Now start thinking. Start concentrating on that right hand. There's nothing else to your body. You see? You forget you got a muscle. There's three things in the world. You see? Just three things and no more. There's your gun with a bullet in it; there's your hand that's going to get the gun out; and there's your target—that door knob, say! Keep on thinking. They ain't any more to your body. You're just a hand and an eye. All your nerves are down there in that hand. They're all piled down there. That hand is full of electricity. Don't let your eyes wander. Keep on concentrating. You're stocking the electricity in that hand. When your hand moves, it'll be as fast as the jump of a spark! And when that hand moves, the gun is going to come out clean in it. It's *got* to come out with it! You hear? It's *got* to! Your finger tips catch under the butt; they flick up. They don't draw the gun; they throw it out of the holster; they pitch the muzzle up, and the butt comes smack back against the palm of your hand. And in the same part of a second you pull the trigger. You hear?"

He leaned forward, trembling from head to

foot. The eyes of the big man were beginning to narrow.

"I hear; I understand!" he said through his teeth.

"You don't pull the gun. You *think* it out of the leather. And then the bullet hits the door knob. You don't move your arm. Your arm doesn't exist. You're just a hand and a brain—thinking! And that thought sends a bullet at the mark!" He leaped back. "Draw!"

There was a wink of light at the hip of Bull Hunter, and the gun roared.

Instantly he cried out, alarmed, confused, ashamed.

"I didn't mean to shoot, Pete. I'm a fool! I didn't mean to! It—I sort of couldn't help it. The—the trigger was just pulled without my wanting it to be! Lord, what'll people think!"

But Pete Reeve had flung his arms around the big man as far as they would go, and he hugged him in a hysteria of joy. Then he leaped back, dancing, throwing up his hands.

"You done it!" he cried, his voice squeaking, hysterical.

"I made a fool of myself, all right," said Bull, bewildered by this exhibition of joy where he had expected anger.

"Fool nothing! Look at that knob!"

The door knob was a smashed wreck, driven into the thick wood of the door by the heavy slug of the revolver. Footsteps were running up the stairs of the hotel. Pete Reeve ran to the door and flung it open.

"It's all right, boys," he called. "Cleaning a gun and it went off. No harm done!"

Chapter Twelve

A Third Party

And now," said Pete Reeve, looking almost rue-
fully at his pupil, "with a little more practice on
that, they ain't a man in the world that could
safely take a chance with you. I couldn't myself."

"Pete!"

"I mean it, son. Not a man in the world. I was
afraid all the time. I was afraid you didn't have
that there electricity in you or whatever they
call it. I was afraid you had too much beef and
not enough nerves. But you haven't. And now
that you have the knack, keep practicing every

141

day—thinking the gun out of the leather—that's the trick!"

Bull Hunter looked down to the gun with great, staring eyes, as though it was the first time in his life that he had seen the weapon. Pete Reeve noted his expression and abruptly became silent, grinning happily, for there was the dawn of a great discovery in the eyes of the big man.

The gun was no longer a gun. It was a part of him. It was flesh of his flesh. He had literally thought it out of the holster, and the report of the weapon had startled him more than it had frightened any one else in the building. He looked in amazement down to the broad expanse of his right hand. It was trembling a little, as though, in fact, that hand were filled with electric currents. He closed his fingers about the butt of the gun. At once the hand became steady as a rock. He toyed with the weapon in loosely opened fingers again, and it slid deftly. It seemed impossible for it to fall into an awkward position.

The voice of Pete Reeve came from a great distance.

"And they's only one thing lacking to make you perfect—and that's to have to fight once for your life—and drop the other gent. After that happens—well, Pete Reeve will have a successor!"

How much that meant Bull Hunter very well knew. The terrible fame of Pete Reeve ran the length and the breadth of the mountains. Of course Bull did not for a moment dream that Pete meant what he said. It was all figurative. It was said to fill him with self-confidence, but part of it was true. He was no longer the clumsy-handed Bull Hunter of the moment before.

A great change had taken place. From that moment his very ways of thinking would be different. He would be capable of less misty movements of the mind. He would be capable of using his brain as fast as his hand acted. A tingle of new life, new possibilities were opening before him. He had always accepted himself as a stupidly hopeless burden in the world, a burden on his friends, useless, cloddish. Now he found that he himself had hopes. His own mind and body was an undiscovered country which he was just beginning to enter. What might be therein was worth a dream or two, and Bull Hunter straightway began to dream, happily. That was a talent which he had always possessed in superabundance.

The brief remainder of the day passed quickly; and then just before supper time a stranger came to call on Pete Reeve. He was a tall, bony fellow with straight-looking eyes and an imperious lift of his head when he addressed any one. Manners was his name—Hugh Manners. When he was introduced he ran his eyes unabashed over the great bulk of Bull Hunter, and then promptly he turned his back on the big man and excluded him from the heart of the conversation. It irritated Bull unwontedly. He discovered that he had changed a great deal from the old days at his uncle's shack when he was used to the scorn and the indifference of all men as a worthless and stupid hulk of flesh, with no mind worth considering, but he said nothing. Another great talent of Bull's was his ability to keep silent.

Shortly after this they went down to the supper table. All through the meal Hugh Manners engaged Pete Reeve in soft, rapid-voiced conversation, which was so nicely gauged as to range that Bull Hunter heard no more than murmurs. He seemed to have a great many important things to say to Pete, and he kept Pete nodding and listening with a frown of serious interest. At first Pete tried to make up for the insolent neglect of his companion by drawing a word or two from Bull from time to time, but it was easy for Bull to see that Pete wished to hear his new-found friend hold forth. It hurt Bull, but he resigned himself and drew out of the talk.

After supper he went up to the room and found a book. There had been little time for reading since he passed the first stages of convalescence from his wounds. Pete Reeve had kept him constantly occupied with gun work, and the hunger for print had been accumulating in Bull. He started to satisfy it now beside the smoking lamp. He hardly heard Pete and Hugh Manners enter the room and go out again onto the second story of the veranda on which their room opened. From time to time the murmur of their voices came to him, but he regarded it not.

It was only when he had lowered the book to muse over a strange sentence that his wandering eye was caught beyond the window by the flash of a falling star of unusual brilliance. It was so bright, indeed, that he crossed the room to look out at the sky, stepping very softly, for he had grown accustomed to lightening his footfall, and now unconsciously the murmuring voices of the talkers made him move stealthily—not to steal upon them, but to keep from breaking in on their talk. But when he came to the door opening on the veranda the words he heard banished all thought of falling stars. He listened, dazed.

Pete Reeve had just broken into the steady flow of the newcomer's talk.

"It's no use, Hugh. I can't go, you see. I'm tied down here with the big fellow."

"Tied down?" thought Bull Hunter, and he winced.

A curse, then: "Why don't you throw the big hulk over?"

"He ain't a hulk," protested Pete somewhat sharply, and the heart of Bull warmed again.

"Hush," said Hugh Manners. "He'll be hearing."

"No danger. He's at his books, and that means that he wouldn't hear a cannon. That's his way."

"He don't look like a book-learned gent," said Hugh Manners with more respect in his voice.

"He don't look like a lot of things that he is," said Pete. "I don't know what he is myself—except that he's the straightest, gentlest, kindest, simplest fellow that ever walked."

Bull Hunter turned to escape from hearing this eulogy, but he dared not move for fear his retreat might be heard—and that would be immensely embarrassing.

"Just what he is I don't know," said Pete again. "He doesn't know himself. He's had what you might call an extra long childhood—that's why he's got that misty look in his eyes."

"That fool look," scoffed Hugh Manners.

"You think so? I tell you, Manners, he's just waking up, and when he's clear waked up he'll be a world-beater! You saw that door knob?"

"Smashed? Yep. What of it."

"He done it—with a gun—standing clean across the room—with a flash draw—shooting from the hip—and he made a clean center hit of it."

Pete brought out these facts jerkily, one by one, piling one extraordinary thing upon the other; and when he had finished Hugh Manners gasped.

"I'm mighty glad," he said, "that you told me that, I—I might of made some mistake."

"You'd sure made an awful mistake if you tangled with him, Manners. Don't forget it."

"Your work, I guess."

"Partly," said Pete modestly. "I speeded his draw up a bit, but he had the straight eye and the steady hand when I started with him. He didn't need much target practice—just the draw."

"And he's really fast?"

"He's got my draw."

That told volumes to Manners.

"And why not take him in with us?" he asked, after a reverent pause.

"Not that!" exclaimed Pete. "Besides, he couldn't ride and keep up with us. He'd wear out three hosses a day with his weight."

"Maybe we could find an extra strong hoss. He ain't so big as to kill a good strong hoss, Pete. I've seen a hoss that carried—"

"No good," said Pete with decision. "I wouldn't even talk to him about our business. He don't guess it. He thinks that I'm—well, he don't have any idea about how I make a living, that's all!"

"But how *will* you make a living if you stick with him?"

"I dunno." Pete sighed. "But I'm not going to turn him down."

"But ain't you about used up your money?"

"It's pretty low."

"And you're supporting him?"

"Sure. He ain't got a cent."

Bull started. He had not thought of that matter at all, but it stood to reason that Pete had expended a large sum on him.

"Sponging?" said Manners cynically.

"Don't talk about it that way," said Pete uneasily. "He's like a big kid. He don't think about those things. If I was broke, he'd give me his last cent."

"That's what you think."

"Shut up, Manners. Bull is like—a cross between a son and a brother."

"Pretty big of bone for your son, Pete. You'll have a hard time supporting him," and Manners chuckled. Then, more seriously: "You're making a fool of yourself, pardner. Throw this big hulk over and come back—with me! They's loads of money staked out waiting for us!"

"Listen," said Pete solemnly. "I'm going to tell you why I'll never turn Bull Hunter down if I live to be a hundred! When I was a kid a dirty trick was done me by old Bill Campbell. I waited all these years till a little while ago to get back at him. Then I found him and fought him. I didn't kill him, but I ruined him and I sent him back to his home tied on his hoss with a busted shoulder that he'll never be able to use again. His right shoulder, at that."

There was a subdued exclamation from Manners, but Pete went on: "Seems he was the uncle of this Bull; took Bull in when Bull was orphaned, because he had to, not because he wanted to, and he raised Bull up to be a sort of general slave around the place. Well, when he comes back home all shot up he tries to get his sons to take my trail, but they didn't have the nerve. But Bull that they'd always looked down on for a big good-for-nothing hulk—Bull stepped out and took my trail on foot and hit across the mountains in a storm, above timber line!

"And he followed till he come up with me here where he found me in jail, accused of a murder. Did he turn back? He didn't. He didn't want the law to hang me. He wanted to kill me with his own hands so's he could go back home and hear his uncle call him a man and praise him a little. That shows how simple he is.

"Well, I'll cut a long story short. Bull scouted around, found out that the sheriff had done the killing himself, and just saddled the blame on me, and then he makes the sheriff confess, gets me out of jail, and takes me out in the woods.

" 'Now,' says he, 'you've got a gun, and I've got a gun, and I'm going to kill you if I can.'

"No use arguing. He goes for his gun. I didn't want to kill a man who'd saved my life. I tried to stop him with bullets. I shot him through the right arm and made him drop his gun. Then he charged me barehanded!"

There was a gasp from Manners.

"Barehanded," repeated Pete. "That's the stuff that's in him! I shot him through the left leg. He pitched onto his face, and then hanged if he didn't get up on one arm and one leg and throw himself at me. He got that big arm of his around me. I couldn't do a thing. My gun was squeezed between him and me. He started fumbling. Pretty soon he found my throat with them big gorilla fingers of his. I thought my last minute had come. One squeeze would have smashed my windpipe—and good-by, Pete Reeve!

"But he wouldn't kill me. After I'd filled him full of lead, he let me go. After he had the advantage he wouldn't take it." Pete choked. He concluded briefly: "He mighty near bled to death before I could get the wounds bandaged, and then I stayed on here and nursed him. Matter of fact, Manners, he saved my life twice and that's why I'm tied to him for life. Besides, between you and me, he means more to me than the rest of the world put together."

"Listen," said Manners, after a pause. "I see what you mean and I'll tell you what you got to do. That big boy will do anything you tell him. He follers you with his eyes. Well, we'll find a hoss that will carry him. I guarantee that. Then you put your game up to him, best foot forward, and he'll come with us."

"Not in a thousand years," said Pete with emotion. "That boy will never go crooked if I can keep him straight. Do you know what he's done? Because his uncle and cousins tried to get me, he's sworn never to see one of 'em again. He's given them up—his own flesh and blood— to follow me, and I'm going to stick to him. That's complete and final."

"No, Pete, of all the fools—"

Bull waited to hear no more. He stole back to the table on the far side of the room sick at heart and sat down to think or to try to think.

The truth came to him slowly. Pete Reeve, whom he had taken as his ideal, was, as a matter of fact—he dared not think what! That blow shook him to the center. But he had been living on the charity of Reeve. He had been draining the resources of the generous fellow. And how would he ever be able to pay him back?

One thing was definite. He must put an end to any increase of the obligations. He must leave.

151

The moment the thought came to him he tore a flyleaf out of the book and wrote in his big, sprawling hand:

> DEAR PETE: I have to tell you that it has just occurred to me that you have been paying all the bills, and I've been paying none. That has to stop, and the only way for me to stop it is to go off all by myself. I hate to sneak away, but if I stay to say good-by I know you'll argue me out of it because I'm no good at an argument. Good-by and good luck, and remember that I'm not forgetting anything that has happened; that when I have enough money to pay you back I'm coming to find you if I have to travel all the way around the world.
>
> Your pardner, BULL.

That done, he paused a moment, tempted to tear up the little slip. But the original impulse prevailed. He put the paper on the table, picked up his hat, and stole slowly from the room.

Chapter Thirteen

Diablo the Terrible

He went out the back door of the hotel so that few people might mark his leaving, and cut for the woods. Once in them, he changed his direction to the east, heading for the lower, rolling hills in that direction. He turned back when the lights of the town had drawn into one small, glimmering ray. Then this, too, went out, and with it the pain of leaving Pete Reeve became acute. He felt lost and alone, that keen mind had guided him so long. As he stalked along with the great swinging stride through the darkness, the holster rubbed on his thigh and he remembered Pete. Truly he had come into the hands of Pete Reeve a child, and he was leaving him as a man.

The dawn found him forty miles away and still swinging strongly down the winding road. It was better country now. The desert sand had disappeared, and here the soil supported a good growth of grass that would fatten the cattle. It was a cheerful country in more ways than the greenness of the grass, however. There were no high mountains, but a continual smooth rolling of hills, so that the landscape varied with every half mile he traveled. And every now and then he had to jump a runlet of water that murmured across his trail.

A pleasant country, a clear sky, and a cool wind touching at his face. The content of Bull Hunter increased with every step he took. He had diminished the sharpness of his hunger by taking up a few links of his belt, but he was glad when he saw smoke twisting over a hill and came, on the other side, in view of a crossroads village. He fingered the few pieces of silver in his pocket. That would be enough for breakfast, at least.

It was enough; barely that and no more, for the long walk had made him ravenous, and the keenness of his spirits served to put a razor edge on an appetite which was already sharp. He began eating before the regular breakfast at the little hotel was ready. He ate while the other men were present. He was still eating when they left.

"How much?" he said when he was done.

His host scratched his head.

"I figure three times a regular meal ought to be about it," he said. "Even then it don't cover everything; but, matter of fact, I'm ashamed to charge any more."

His ruefulness changed to a grin when he had the money in his hand, and Bull Hunter rose from the table.

"But you got something to feed, son," he said. "You certainly got something to feed. And—is what the boys are saying right?"

It came to Bull that while he sat at the table there had been many curious glances directed toward him, and a humming whisper had passed around the table more than once. But he was accustomed to these side glances and murmurs, and he had paid no attention. Besides, food had been before him.

"I don't know. What do they say?"

"That you're Dunbar from the South—Hal Dunbar."

"That's not my name," said Bull. "My name is Hunter."

"I guessed they was wrong," said the other. "Trouble is, every time anybody sees a big man they say: 'There goes Hal Dunbar.' But you're too big even to be Dunbar, I reckon."

He surveyed the bulk of Bull Hunter with admiring respect. This personal survey embarrassed the big man. He would have withdrawn, but his host followed with his conversation.

"We know Dunbar is coming up this way, though. He sent the word on up that he's going to come to ride 'Diablo.' I guess you've heard about Diablo?"

Bull averred that he had not, and his eyes went restlessly down the road. It wove in long curves, delightfully white with the bordering of green on either side. He could see it almost tossing among the far-off hills. Now was the time of all times for walking, and if Pete Reeve started to trail him this morning, he would need to put as much distance behind him by night as his long legs could cover. But still the hotel proprietor hung beside him. He wanted to make the big man talk. It was possible that there might be in him a story as big as his body.

"So you ain't heard of Diablo? Devil is the right name for him. Black as night and meaner'n a mountain lion. That's Diablo. He's big enough and strong enough to carry even you. Account of him being so strong, that's why Dunbar wants him."

"Big enough and strong enough to carry me?" repeated Bull Hunter.

He had had unfortunate experiences trying to ride horses. His weight crushed down their quarters and made them walk with braced legs. To be sure, that was up in the high mountains where the horses were little more than ponies.

"Yep. Big enough. He's kind of a freak hoss, you see. Runs to almost seventeen hands, I've heard tell, though I ain't seen him. He's over to the Bridewell place yonder in the hills—along about fifteen miles by the road, I figure. He run till he was three without ever being taken up, and he got wild as a mustang. They never was good on managing on the Bridewell place, you see? And then when they tried to break him he started doing some breaking on his own account. They say he can jump about halfway to the sky and come down stiff-legged in a way that snaps your neck near off. I seen young Huniker along about a month after he tried to ride Diablo. Huniker was a pretty good rider, by all accounts, but he was sure a sick gent around hosses after Diablo got through with him. Scared of a ten-year-old mare, Huniker was, after Diablo finished with him. Scot Porter tried him, too. That was a fight! Lasted close onto an hour, they say, nip and tuck all the way. Diablo wasn't bucking all the time. No, he ain't that way. He waits in between spells till he's thought up something new to do. And he's always thinking, they say. But if he wasn't so mean he'd be a wonderful hoss. Got a stride as long as from here to that shed, they say."

He rambled on with a growing enthusiasm.

"And think of a hoss like that being given away!"

"Given away?" said Bull with a sudden interest.

And then he remembered that horses were outside of his education entirely.

He listened with gloomy attention while his host went on: "Yes, sir. Given away is what I said and given away is what I mean. Old Chick Bridewell has kept him long enough, he says. He's tired of paying buckaroos for getting busted up trying to ride that hoss. Man-eater, that's what he calls Diablo, and he wants to give the hoss away to the first man that can ride him. Hal Dunbar heard about it and sent up word that he was coming up to ride him."

"He must be a brave man," said Bull innocently. He had an immense capacity for admiring others.

"Brave?" The proprietor paused as though this had not occurred to him before. "Why, they ain't such a thing as fear in Hal Dunbar, I guess. But if he decides to ride Diablo, he'll ride him, well enough. He has his way about things, Hal Dunbar does."

The sketchy portrait impressed Bull Hunter greatly. "You know him, then?"

"How'd I be mistaking you for him if I knowed him? No, he lives away down south, but they's a pile heard about him that's never seen him."

For some reason the words of his host remained in the mind of Bull as he went down the road that day. Oddly enough, he pictured man and horse as being somewhat alike—Diablo vast and black and fierce, and Hal Dunbar dark and huge and terrible of eye, also; which was proof enough that Bull Hunter was a good deal of a child. He cared less about the world as it was than for the world as it might be, and as long as life gave him something to dream about, he did not care in the least about the facts of existence.

Another man would have been worried about the future; but Bull Hunter went down the road with his swinging stride, perfectly at peace with himself and with life. He had not enough money in his pocket to buy a meal, but he was not thinking so far ahead.

It was still well before noon when he came in sight of the Bridewell place. It varied not a whit from the typical ranch of that region, a low-built collection of sheds and arms sprawling around the ranch house itself. About the building was a farflung network of corrals. Bull Hunter found his way among them and followed a sound of hammering. He was well among the sheds when a great black stallion shot into view around a nearby corner, tossing his head and mane. He was pursued by a shrill voice crying: "Diablo! Hey! You old fool! Stand still—it's me—it's Tod!"

To the amazement of Bull Hunter, Diablo the Terrible, Diablo the man-killer, paused and reluctantly turned about, shaking his head as though he did not wish to obey but was compelled by the force of conscience. At once a bare-legged boy of ten came in sight, running and shaking his fist angrily at the giant horse. Indeed, it was a tremendous animal. Not the seventeen hands that the hotel proprietor had described to Bull, but a full sixteen three, and so proudly high-headed, so stout-muscled of body, so magnificently long and tapering of leg, that a wiser horseman than the hotel keeper might have put Diablo down for more than seventeen hands.

Most tall horses are like tall men—they are freakish and malformed in some of their members; but Diablo was as trim as a pony. He had the high withers, the mightily sloped shoulders, and the short back of a weight carrier. And although at first glance his underpinning seemed too frail to bear the great mass of his weight or withstand the effort of his driving power of shoulders and deep, broad thighs, yet a closer reckoning made one aware of the comfortable dimensions of the cannon bone with all that this feature portended. Diablo carried his bulk with the grace which comes of compacted power well in hand.

Not that Bull Hunter analyzed the stallion in any such fashion. He was, literally, ignorant of horseflesh. But in spite of his ignorance the long neck, not overfleshed, suggested length of stride and the mighty girth meant wind beyond exhaustion and told of the great heart within. The points of an ordinary animal may be overlooked, but a great horse speaks for himself in every language and to every man. He was coal black, this Diablo, except for the white stocking of his off forefoot; he was night black, and so silken sleek that, as he turned and pranced, flashes of light glimmered from shoulders to flanks.

Bull Hunter stared in amazement that changed to appreciation, and appreciation that burst in one overpowering instant to the full understanding of the beauty of the horse. Joy entered the heart of the big man. He had looked on horses hitherto as pretty pictures perhaps, but useless to him. Here was an animal that could bear him like the wind wherever he would go. Here was a horse who could gallop tirelessly under him all day and labor through the mountains, bearing him as lightly as the cattle ponies bore ordinary men. The cumbersome feeling of his own bulk, which usually weighed heavily on

Bull, disappeared. He felt light of heart and light of limb.

In the meantime the bare-legged boy had come to the side of the big horse, still shrilling his anger. He stood under the lofty head of the stallion and shook his small fist into the face of Diablo the Terrible. And while Bull, quaking, expected to see the head torn from the shoulders of the child, Diablo pointed his ears and sniffed the fist of the boy inquisitively.

In fact, this could not be the horse of which the hotel keeper had told him. Or perhaps he had been recently tamed and broken?

That, for some reason, made the heart of Bull Hunter sink.

The boy now reached up and twisted his fingers into the mane of the black.

"Come along now. And if you pull away ag'in, you old fool, Diablo, I'll give you a thumping, I tell you. Git along!"

Diablo meekly lowered his head and made his step mincing to regulate his gait to that of his tiny master. He was brought alongside a rail fence. There he waited patiently while the child climbed up to the top rail and then slid onto his back. Again Bull Hunter caught his breath. He expected to see the stallion leap into the air and snap the child high above his head with a single arching of his back, but there was no such violent reaction. Diablo, indeed, turned his head with his ears flattened and bared his teeth, but it was only to snort at the knee of the boy. Plainly he was bluffing, if horses ever bluffed. The boy carelessly dug his brown toes into the cheek of the great horse and shoved his head about.

"Giddap," he called. "Git along, Diablo!"

Diablo walked gently forward.

"Hurry up! I ain't got all day!" And the boy thumped the giant with his bare heels.

Diablo broke into a trot as soft, as smooth flowing, as water passing over a smooth bed of sand. Bull ran to the corner of the shed and gaped after them until the pair slid around a corner and were gone. Instinctively he drew off his hat and gaped.

He was startled back to himself by loud laughter nearby, and, looking up, he saw an old fellow in overalls with a handful of nails and a hammer. He stood among a scattering of uprights which represented, apparently, the beginnings of the skeleton of a big barn. Now he leaned against one of these uprights and indulged his mirth. Bull regarded him mildly; he was used to being laughed at.

Chapter Fourteen

The Bargain

That's the way they all do," said the old man.

"They all gape the same fool way when they see Diablo the first time."

"Is that the wild horse?" asked Bull in his gentle voice.

"That's him. I s'pose after seeing Tod handle him, you'll want to try to ride him right off?"

Bull looked in the direction in which the horse had disappeared. He swallowed a lump that had risen in his throat and shook his head sadly.

"Nope. You see, I dunno nothing about horses, really."

The old man regarded him with a new and sudden interest.

"Takes a wise man to call himself a fool," he declared axiomatically.

Bull took this dubious bit of praise as an invitation and came slowly closer to the other. He had the child's way of eying a stranger with embarrassing steadiness at a first meeting and thereafter paying little attention to the face. He wrote the features down in his memory and kept them at hand for reference, as it were. As he drew nearer, the old man grew distinctly serious, and when Bull was directly before him he gazed up into the face of Bull with distinct amazement. At a distance the big man did not seem so large because of the grace of his proportions; when he was directly confronted, however, he seemed a veritable giant.

"By the Lord, you *are* big. And who might you be, stranger?"

"My name's Charlie Hunter; though mostly folks call me just plain Bull."

"That's queer," chuckled the other. "Well, glad to know you. I'm Bridewell."

They shook hands, and Bridewell noted the gentleness of the touch of the giant. As a rule strong men are tempted to show their strength when they shake hands; Bridewell appreciated the modesty of Charlie Hunter.

"And you didn't come to ride Diablo?"

"No. I just stopped in to see him. And—" Bull sighed profoundly.

"I know. He gives even me a touch now and then, though I know what a devil he is!"

"Devil?" repeated Bull, astonished. "Why, he's as gentle as a kitten!"

"Because you seen Tod ride him?" Bridewell laughed. "That don't mean nothing. Tod can bully him, sure. But just let a grown man come near him—with a saddle! That'll change things pretty pronto! You'll see the finest little bit of boiled down hell-raising that ever was! The jingle of a pair of spurs is Diablo's idea of a drum— and he makes his charge right off! Gentle? Huh!" The grunt was expressive. "And what good's a hoss if he can't be rode with a saddle?" He waved the subject of Diablo into the distance. "They ain't any hope unless Hal Dunbar can ride him. If he can't, I'll shoot the beast!"

"Shoot him?" echoed Bull Hunter. He took a pace back, and his big, boyish face clouded to a frown. "Not that, I guess!"

"Why not?" asked Bridewell, curious at the change in the big stranger. "Why not? What good is he?"

"Why—he's good just to look at. I'd keep him just for that."

"And you can have him just for that—if you can manage to handle him. Want to try?"

Bull shook his head. "I don't know nothing

about horses," he confessed again. He glanced at the skeleton of standing beams. "Building a barn, eh?"

"You wouldn't call it pitching hay or shoeing a hoss that I'm doing, I guess," said the old fellow crossly. "I'm fussing at building a barn, but a fine chance I got. I get all my timber here—look at that!"

He indicated the stacks of beams and lumber around him.

"And then I get some men out of town to work with me on it. But they get lonely. Don't like working on a ranch. Besides, they had a scrap with me. I wouldn't have 'em loafing around the job. Rather have no help at all than have a loafer helping me. So they quit. Then I tried to get my cow hands to give me a lift, but they wouldn't touch a hammer. Specialists in cows is what they say they are, ding bust 'em! So here I am trying to do something and doing nothing. How can I handle a beam that it takes three men to lift?"

He illustrated by going to a stack of long and massive timbers and tugging at the end of one of them. He was able to raise that end only a few inches.

"You see?"

Bull nodded.

"Suppose you give me the job handling the timbers?" he suggested. "I ain't much good with a hammer and nails, but I might manage the lifting."

"All by yourself? One man?" He eyed the bulk of Bull hopefully for a moment, then the light faded from his face. "Nope, you couldn't raise 'em. Not them joists yonder!"

"I think I could," said Bull.

Old Bridewell thrust out his jaw. He had been a combative man in his youth; and he still had the instinct of a fighter.

"I got ten dollars," he said, "that says you can't lift that beam and put her up on end! That one right there that I tried to lift a minute ago!"

"All right," Bull nodded.

"You're on for that bet?" the old man chuckled gayly. "All right. Let's see you give a heave!"

Bull Hunter obediently stepped to the timber. It was a twelve footer of bulky dimensions, heavy wood not thoroughly seasoned. Yet he did not approach one end of it. He laid his immense hands on the center of it. Old Bridewell chuckled to himself softly as he watched; he was beginning to feel that the big stranger was a little simple-minded. His chuckling ceased when he saw the timber cant over on one edge.

"Look out!" he called, for Bull had slipped his hand under the lifted side. "You'll get your fingers smashed plumb off that way."

"I have to get a hold under it, you see," explained Bull calmly, and so saying his knees sagged a little and when they straightened the timber rose lightly in his hands and was placed on his shoulder.

"Where'd you like to have it?" asked Bull.

Bridewell rubbed his eyes. "Yonder," he said faintly.

Bull walked to the designated place, the great timber teetering up and down, quivering with the jar of each stride. There he swung one end to the ground and thrust the other up until it was erect.

"Is this the way you want it?" said Bull.

By this time Bridewell had recovered his self-possession to some degree, yet his eyes were wide as he approached.

"Yep. Just let it lean agin' that corner piece, will you, Hunter?"

Bull obeyed.

"That might make a fellow's shoulder sort of sore," he remarked, "if he had to carry those timbers all day."

"All day?" gasped Bridewell, and then he saw that the giant, indeed, was not even panting from his effort. He was already turning his attention to the pile of timbers.

"Here," he said, reluctantly drawing out some money. "Here's your ten."

But Bull refused it. "Can't take it," he explained. "I just made the bet by way of talk. You see, I knew I could lift it; and you didn't have any real idea about me. Besides, if I'd lost I couldn't have paid. I haven't any money."

He said this so gravely and simply that old Bridewell watched him quizzically, half suspecting that there was a touch of irony hidden somewhere. It gradually dawned on him that a man who was flat broke was refusing money which he had won fairly on a bet. The idea staggered Bridewell. He was within an ace of putting Bull Hunter down as a fool. Something held him back, through some underlying respect for the physical might of the big man and a respect, also, for the honesty which looked out of his eyes. He pocketed the money slowly. He was never averse to saving.

"But I've been thinking," said Bull, as he sadly watched the money disappear, "that you might be needing me to help you put up the barn? Do you think you could hire me?"

"H'm," grumbled Bridewell. "You think you could handle these big timbers all day?"

"Yes," said Bull, "if none of 'em are any bigger than that last one. Yes, I could handle 'em all day easily."

It was impossible to doubt that he said this judiciously and not with a desire to overstate his powers. In spite of himself the old rancher believed.

"You see," explained Bull eagerly, "you said

that you needed three men for that work. That's why I ask."

"And I suppose you'd want the pay of three men?"

Bull shook his head. "Anything you want to pay me," he declared.

The rancher frowned. This sounded like the beginning of a shrewd bargain, and his respect and suspicion were equally increased.

"Suppose you say what you want?" he asked.

"Well," Bull said slowly, "I'd have to have a place to sleep. And—I'm a pretty big eater."

"I guess you are," said Bridewell. "But if you do three men's work you got a right to three men's food. What else do you want?"

Bull considered, as though there were few other wishes that he could express. "I haven't any money," he apologized. "D'you think maybe you could pay me a little something outside of food and a place to sleep?"

Bridewell blinked, and then prepared himself to become angry, when it dawned on him that this was not intended for sarcasm. He found that Bull was searching his face eagerly, as though he feared that he were asking too much.

"What would do you?" suggested Bridewell tentatively.

"I dunno," said Bull, sighing with relief. "Anything you think."

It was plain that the big man was half-witted—or nearly so. Bridewell kept the sparkle of exultation out of his eyes.

"You leave it to me, then, and I'll do what's more'n right by you. When d'you want to start work?"

"Right now."

Chapter Fifteen

Crackajack Pals

When Bull left the dining room that night after supper, Mrs. Bridewell looked across the table at her husband with horror in her eyes.

"Did you see?" she gasped. "He ate that *whole* pot of beans!"

"Sure I seen," and he grinned.

"But—he'll eat us out of house and home! Why, he's like a wolf!"

Bridewell chuckled with superior knowledge. "He's ate enough for three," he admitted, "but he's worked enough for six—besides, most of his wages come in food. But work? I never seen anything like it! He handled more timbers than a dozen. When it come to spiking them in place he seen me swinging that twelve-pound sledge and near breaking my back. 'I think it's easier this way,' he says. 'Besides you can hit a lot faster if you just use one hand.' And he takes the hammer, and sends that big spike in all the way to the head with one lick. And he wondered why I didn't work the same way! Ain't got any idea how strong he is."

Mrs. Bridewell listened with wide eyes. "The idea," she murmured. "The idea! Where's he now?"

Her husband went to the back door. "He's sitting over by the pump talking to Tod. Sitting talking like they was one age. I reckon he's sort of half-witted."

"How come?" sharply asked Mrs. Bridewell. "Ain't Tod got more brains than most growed-up men?"

"I reckon he has," admitted the proud father.

And if they had put the same question to Bull Hunter, the giant would have agreed with them emphatically. He approached the child tamer of Diablo with a diffidence that was almost reverence. The freckle-faced boy looked up from his whittling when the shadow of Bull fell athwart him, with an equal admiration; also with suspicion, for the cow-punchers, on the whole, were apt to make game of the youngster and his grave, grown-up ways. He was, therefore, shrewdly suspicious of jests at his expense.

Furthermore, he had seen the big stranger heaving the great timbers about and whirling the sledge with one hand; he half suspected that the jokes might be pointed with the weight of that heavy hand. His amazement was accordingly great when he found the big man actually sitting down beside him, cross-legged, and he was absolutely stupefied when Bull Hunter said: "I've been aiming at this chance to talk to you, Tod, all day."

"H'm," grunted Tod noncommittally, and examined the other with a cautious side glance.

But the face of Bull Hunter was unutterably free from guile. Tod instantly began to adjust himself. The men he most worshiped were the lean, swift, profanely formidable cowpunchers. But there was something in him that responded with a thrill to this accepted equality with such a man as Bull Hunter. Even his father he had seen stricken to an awed silence at the sight of Bull's prowess.

"You see," explained Bull frankly, "I been wondering how you managed to handle Diablo the way you do."

Tod chuckled. "It's just a trick. You watch me a while with him, you'll soon catch on."

But Bull shook his head as he answered: "Maybe a mighty bright man might figure it out, but I'm not good at figuring things out, Tod."

The boy blinked. He was accustomed to the studied understatement of the cow-punchers and he was accustomed, also, to their real vanity which underlay the surface shyness. But it was patent that Bull Hunter, in spite of his size, was truly humble. This conception was new to Tod and slowly grew in his brain. His active eyes ran over the bulk beside him; he almost pitied the giant.

"Besides," pondered Bull heavily, "I guess there's a whole lot of bright men that have seen you handle Diablo, but they couldn't make out what you did. They tried to ride Diablo and got their necks nearly broken. They were good riders, but I'm not. You see, Diablo's the first horse I've ever seen that could really carry me." He added apologetically: "I'm so heavy."

No vanity, certainly. He gestured toward himself as though he were ashamed of his brawn, and the heart of Tod warmed and expanded. He himself would never be large, and his heart had ached because of his smallness many a time.

"Yep," he said judiciously, "you're pretty heavy. About the heaviest I ever seen, I guess. Maybe Hal Dunbar is as big, but I never seen Hal."

"I've heard a good deal about Hal, but—"

He stopped short and stiffened. Tod saw that the eyes of the big man had fixed on the corral in which stood Diablo. A puff of wind had come, and the great black had thrown up his head into it, an imposing picture with mane and tail blown sidewise. Not until the stallion turned away from the unseen thing which he had scented in the wind, did Bull turn to his small companion with a sigh.

Tod nodded, his eyes glinting. "I know," he said. "I used to feel that way—before I learned how to handle Diablo." He interpreted: "You feel like it'd be pretty fine to get onto Diablo's back and have him gallop under you."

"About the finest thing in the world," sighed Bull Hunter. He cast out his great hands before him as he tried to explain the mysterious emotions which the horse had excited in him. "You see, Tod, I'm pretty big and I'm pretty slow. Most folks have horses, and they get about pretty lively on 'em, but I've always had to walk."

The enormity of this lack made Tod stare, for travel and horses were inseparably connected in his mind. He shuddered a little at the thought of the big man stalking across the burning and interminable sands of the desert or toiling through the mountains. It seemed to him that he could see the signs of that pain stamped in the face of Bull Hunter, and his heart leaped again in sympathy.

"So when I saw Diablo—" Bull paused. But

Tod had understood. Suddenly the boy became excited.

"Suppose you was to learn to ride Diablo before Hal Dunbar come to try him out? Suppose that?"

"Could you teach me?" the giant asked in an almost awed whisper.

The child looked over his companion with a vague wonder. It would be a tremendous responsibility, this teaching of the giant, but what could be more spectacular than to have such a man as his pupil? But to share his unique empire over Diablo—that would be a great price to pay!

"No," he decided, "it wouldn't do. Besides, suppose even I *could* teach you how to ride Diablo—with a saddle, which I don't think I could—what would happen when Hal Dunbar come up to these parts and found that the hoss he wanted was somebody else's? He'd make an awful fuss—and he's a fighting man, Bull."

He said this impressively, leaning a little toward the giant, and he was rewarded infinitely by seeing the right hand of the giant stir a little toward the holster at his thigh.

"I guess I'd have to take my chance with him," was all Bull answered in his mildest tone.

Tod was beginning to guess that there was a certain amount of mental strength under this quiet exterior. He had often noted that his father, who made by far the most noise, was more easily placated than his mother, in spite of her gentle silences. The strength of Bull Hunter had a strain of the same thing about it.

"You'd take a chance with Hal Dunbar?" he repeated wonderingly. He trembled a little, with a sort of nervous ecstasy at the thought of that coming encounter. "That's more'n anybody else in these parts would do. Why, everybody's heard about Hal Dunbar. Everybody's scared of him. He can ride anything that's big enough to carry him; he can fight like a wildcat with his hands; and he can shoot—like"—his eye wandered toward a superlative—"like Pete Reeve, almost," he concluded with a tone of awe.

A spark of tenderness shone in the eye of Bull. "D'you know Pete Reeve?"

"No, and I don't want to. Ma had a brother once, and he met up with Pete Reeve."

A tragedy was inferred in that oblique reference. Bull decided that this was a conversational topic on which he must remain silent, and yet he yearned to speak of the little withered catlike fellow with the wise brain which had done so much for him.

"When I'm big enough," mused the boy with a quiet savagery, "maybe I'll meet up with Pete Reeve."

Bull switched the talk to a more comfortable

topic. "But how'd you make a start with that man-eating Diablo?"

Tod studied the question. "I got a way with hosses, you see," he began modestly.

He played two brown fingers in his mouth and sent out a shrilling whistle that was answered immediately by a whinny, and a little chestnut gelding, sun-faded to a sand color nearly, cantered into view around the corner of a shed and approached them. He came to a pause near by, and having studied Bull Hunter with large, unafraid, curious eyes for a moment, began to nibble impertinently at the ragged hat brim of the child.

"Git away!" exclaimed Tod, and when the chestnut made no move to go, the brown fist flashed up at the reaching head. But the head was jerked away with a motion of catlike deftness.

"He's a terrible bother, Crackajack is," said the boy angrily, and from the corner of his eye he stole a glance of unspeakable pride at the big man.

"He's a beauty," exclaimed Bull Hunter. "A regular beauty!"

For Crackajack combined the toughness of a mustang and the lean, strong running lines of a thoroughbred in miniature. His legs were as delicately made as the legs of a deer; his head was a little model of impish intelligence and beauty.

"You and Crackajack are pals," said Bull. "I guess that's what you are!"

"We get on tolerable well," admitted the boy, whose heart was full with this praise of his pet.

Bull continued on the agreeable topic: "And I'll bet he's fast, too. He looks like speed to me!"

"Maybe you don't know hosses, but you sure got hoss sense." Tod chuckled. "Most folks take Crackajack for a toy pony. He ain't. I've seen him carry a full-grown man all day and keep up with the best of 'em. He don't mind the weight of me no more'n if I was a feather. He's fast, he's tough, and he knows more'n a hoss should know, you might say!"

He changed his voice, and a brief command made Crackajack give up his teasing and retreat. Bull watched the exquisite little creature go, with a smile of pleasure. He did not know it, but that smile unlocked the last door to Tod's heart.

"He was pretty near as wild as Diablo when I first got him," said the boy. "And mean—say, he'd been kicked around all his life. But I fatted him up in the barn, and he got so's he'd follow me around. And now he runs loose like a dog and comes when I whistle. He knows more things than you could shake a stick at, Crackajack does."

"I'll bet he does," said Bull with shining eyes.

"Say," said the boy suddenly, "I'm going to tell you about the way I worked with Diablo."

"I'll take that mighty kind," said Bull gratefully. "D'you think I'd have a chance with him even if you showed me how?"

"You got to have a way with hosses," admitted the boy, and he examined Bull again. "But I think you'll get on with hossflesh pretty well. When Diablo first come, he used to go plumb crazy when anybody come near his corral. He still does if a growed man comes there. Well, they used to go out and stand and watch him and laugh at him prancing around and kicking up a fuss at the sight of 'em. And it made me mad. Made me plumb mad to see them bother Diablo when he wasn't doing no harm, when they wasn't gaining anything by it, either.

"I used to go out when nobody was around and stand by the bars with a bit of hay and grain heads in my hand. First off he'd prance around even at me, but pretty soon he seen that I wasn't big enough to do him no harm, and then he'd just stand still and snort and look at me. Along about the third time he took notice of the grain heads and come and smelled them, and the next day he ate 'em.

"Well, I kept at it that way. Pretty soon I went inside the corral. Diablo just come up sort of excited and trembling and didn't know whether to bash my head in with his forehoofs or let me go. Then he seen the grain heads and ate them while he was making up his mind what to do about me. And he winded up by just having a little talk with me. He was terrible dirty and dusty, and he was shedding. Nobody dared to brush him, and so I took a soft-haired brush and started to work on his neck. He liked it, and so I dressed him down and left him pretty near shining. And every day after that I went and had a talk with him and brushed him. Then I rode Crackajack up to the bars and let Diablo see me on him, with no bridle or saddle. Pretty soon I found out that it was the saddle and the bridle and the spurs that scared Diablo to death. He didn't mind anything else so very much. So one day I climbed up the fence and slid onto Diablo's back, and he just turned his head and snorted at me. Just then pa seen me and let out a terrible yell, and Diablo pitched me right off over his head and over the fence. But I got right up and come back to him. He seen that he could get me off whenever he wanted to and he seen that I didn't do him no harm when I got on.

"After that everything was easy. I never bothered him none with a saddle or a bridle. And there you are. D'you think you can do the same?"

"But the saddle and the bridle?" said Bull. "What about them?"

183

"That's up to you to figure out a way of getting him used to 'em. I'll go introduce you now, if I can."

Bull rose, and the boy led the way.

"If he takes to you pretty kind," said the boy, "you may have a chance. But if he begins acting up, it won't be no use."

Chapter Sixteen

The Test

Diablo greeted them with a throwing up of his formidable head. He took his place in the very middle of his corral, but when Bull Hunter and his small guide reached the bars, the black stallion seemed to go suddenly mad. He flung himself into the air and came down bucking. Back and forth across the corral he threw himself in the wildest swirl of pitching that Bull Hunter had ever seen or ever dreamed of.

"He's an educated bucker, you see?" said the boy in admiration. "They ain't any trick that he don't know. Look!"

Diablo had begun to sunfish in the most approved method, and swirled from this to some fence rowing as swift as the jagged course of lightning. At every jump Bull could see an imaginary rider snapped from the back of the black giant. A cloud of dust was sent swishing up, and in the midst of this fog, Diablo came to a pause as sudden as the beginning of his strange struggle against an imaginary foeman; but it seemed to Bull Hunter that the ground beneath his feet was still quivering from the impacts of that mighty body.

"That's just his way of telling you what he'll do when you try to saddle him," chuckled the boy.

As he spoke he slipped through the bars of the corral.

"Look out!" exclaimed Bull in horror, for the stallion had rushed at the small intruder with gaping mouth. Bull reached for his gun—Diablo was already on the child, but at the last minute he swerved, and flashed around Tod in a circle.

"He's all right," Tod was shrilling through his laughter, for the horrified face of Bull amused him. "That's just his way of saying that he's glad to see me!"

In fact, Diablo came to a sudden halt directly behind the child, his head towering aloft above that of Tod while he flashed his defiance at Bull Hunter, as though he were making use of the small bulwark of Tod against the stranger.

"Diablo, you old fool," the boy was saying, as he reached up and managed to wind his fingers in the end of Diablo's mane, "you come along and meet my friend, Bull Hunter. I figure you're going to get to know him pretty good before long. Hey, Bull, come up close to the bars so's he can see you ain't got a rope or a whip or spurs, and stick your hand out so's he can sniff at it. That's his way of saying how d'ye do."

Bull obeyed, and to his amazement, Diablo responded to the small forward urge of the child's hand and approached the bars one trembling step at a time. Bull began to talk to him softly. He had never talked like this to any living creature. He did not know exactly what he said. The words came of their own accord into his throat. He only knew that he wanted to reassure the big, powerful, uncertain brute, and though Diablo stopped short at the first sound of Bull's voice and laid his ears back, he presently pricked one of those ears again and allowed himself to be drawn forward with long, crouching strides.

"That's the way!" said the child softly, as though he feared that a loud voice might break in upon the spell. "You know how to talk to him! And, outside of me, you're the only one that does! I knew you'd have it in you!"

For Diablo had extended his long neck and

actually sniffed the hand of Bull Hunter. He immediately tossed his head aloft, but he did not flinch away.

"That's half the fight won already," advised the boy in the same soft voice. "D'you want to try the saddle on him now?"

"The saddle? Now?" exclaimed Bull. "I should say not! Why, he don't hardly know me; I'll have to get acquainted before I try anything like that."

He discovered that Tod was nodding in hearty approval.

"You do know," he said. "Don't tell me that you ain't been around hosses a pile. Yep, you got to get acquainted. What you want to do now?"

Bull considered. "I'd like to have something to show him that it isn't unpleasant having me around. I'd like to have him see some good results, you know? Is there anything I could feed him?"

The boy chuckled. "Best thing is some dried prunes with the seeds taken out of 'em. I have some at the house. They get stuck in Diablo's teeth and it's sure funny to see him eat 'em. But he just nacherally plumb likes the taste of them prunes."

He followed his own suggestion by scampering away to the house and returned almost at once with a hat full of the prunes.

"You want to feed him these now?"

"First," said Bull, "I'd like to have you leave us alone. If I can't teach him to like me all by myself, then I'd better give up right away."

The boy looked at him in surprise and then impulsively stretched out his hand. They shook hands gravely.

"You got the right idea, pardner," said Tod. "Go ahead—and good luck! And keep talking to him all the time. That's the main thing!"

He retreated accordingly, but before the evening was over, Bull regretted dismissing his little ally so quickly, for although Diablo indulged in no more threatening outbreaks of temper, he resolutely refused to eat the prunes from Bull's hand. Several times he approached the bars of the corral and the patiently extended hand, but always he drew back, snorting, and sometimes he would run around the corral, shaking his head and throwing up his heels after the manner of a horse tempted but still afraid of being overruled.

It was long after dark when Bull gave up the attempt. He went back to the bunk house, rolled up the blankets which had been assigned to him, and carried them out to the corral. Close to the fence he laid them down, and a few minutes later he was wrapped in them and sound asleep. The last thing he remembered was the form of the great stallion, standing watchfully in the exact middle of the corral, the starlight glimmering very faintly in his big eyes.

Bull Hunter fell asleep and had a nightmare of the arrival of the famous Hal Dunbar the next day, a fierce conquest of Diablo, and the battle ending with the departure of Dunbar on the back of the stallion.

The dream waked him, nervous, and he turned and saw Diablo standing huge and formidable in the darkness, as though he had not moved from his first position.

In the morning the arduous labors of the building began again, and though the prodigious appetite of Bull at the breakfast table made even old Bridewell look askance, Bull had not been at work an hour handling the ponderous uprights and joists before his employer was smiling to himself. His new hand was certainly worth his keep, and more, for weariness seemed a stranger to that big body, and no weight was too great to be cheerily assumed. And always he worked with a sort of nervous anxiety as though he feared that he might not be doing enough.

During the day Bridewell attempted to probe the past history of his hired man, expecting a story as big as the body of the man, but Bull was discreetly vague, for he had no wish to reveal his connection with Pete Reeve; and if he left out Reeve he felt that there was nothing in his life worth talking about. Many a time he wondered what the little gunfighter was doing, and what trail he was riding now. A dangerous trail, he doubted not, and a lawless trail, he greatly feared. But some day he might be able to find the terrible little man and bring him back to a truer place in society.

That night he began again the long, quiet struggle with Diablo; and before he ended, Diablo had gathered some of the dried fruit from the palm of his hand with a sensitive, trembling pair of lips. And he had come back for more, and more. Yet it was not until the next night that Bull ventured inside the bars of the corral and sat cross-legged on the ground, with a vague feeling that Diablo would be less alarmed if his visitor bulked less large.

Inside the bars he seemed an entirely new proposition to the stallion. The big black kept discreetly on the far side of the corral with much snorting and stamping, and it was not until the next evening that he ventured to approach the man. Still another day passed before Bull was allowed to stand and touch the neck of the black; and that, it seemed to him, was the greatest forward step toward the conquest.

It was terribly slow work, and in the meantime the skeleton frame of the barn was fast rising. Would he accomplish his purpose by the time the barn was completed and Bridewell no longer had a use for him? Or would Hal Dunbar arrive before that appointed time? That night, however, another portentous event happened. Waking in the night, Bull heard a sound of deep, regular breathing close to him, and, turning on his side, he saw that Diablo had lain down as close to him as the corral fence would allow, and there he slept, panther-black, sleek in the starlight. Bull stretched out his hand. The head of the stallion jerked up, but a moment later he carelessly sniffed the extended fingers and resumed his position of repose. And the heart of Bull Hunter swelled with triumph.

That event gave him a new idea, and the following evening he made a groundwork of branches in the corner of the corral itself, and put down his blankets on the evergreens. Diablo was much concerned and walked about examining the new work from every angle. There Bull slept, and the next night he found that during the day the stallion had torn the boughs to pieces and scattered them about. He patiently laid a new foundation, and after this the bed was left strictly alone.

In the meantime Bull had made a light, strong halter of rawhide, and after several attempts he managed to slip it onto the head of Diablo. Once in place, it was easy to teach Diablo that he must follow when he felt a pull on the halter—the first steps were rewarded with dried prunes, and after that it was simple.

On that evening, also, Bull made his next step forward toward the most difficult proposition of all—he took a partly filled barley sack and put it on the back of Diablo. The next moment the sack was shot into the air as Diablo leaped up and arched his back like a cat at the height of his leap.

He came down trembling and snorting, but Bull picked up the fallen sack and allowed him to smell it. Diablo found that the smell was good and that the hateful sack even contained things very good to eat. The next time the sack was put on his back he quivered and shrank, but he did not buck it off.

After that, Bull spent his evenings in gradually increasing the weight of that sack until a full hundred pounds caused Diablo no worry whatever, and when this point had been attained, Bull decided that he might venture his own bulk on the back of Diablo. He confided his purpose to Tod, and the boy, greatly excited, hid himself at a distance to watch.

In the beginning it was deceptively easy. Diablo stood perfectly unconcerned as Bull raised himself on the bars of the fence. And when the long legs of Bull was passed over his back, Diablo merely turned his head and sniffed the shoe tentatively. Slowly, very softly, steadying himself on the top bar of the fence, Bull lowered his weight more and more until the whole burden was on the back of the stallion—and then he took his hands from the top rail.

But the moment he released that grip there was a change in Diablo, as though he realized that the man had suddenly trusted himself entirely to his mount, Bull felt a sudden wincing of all that great body; the quarters sank and trembled. He thought at first that it was because the horse was failing under the weight of this ponderous burden; but instinct told him a moment later that it was fear, and a mixture of suspicious anger.

Diablo took one of his long, catlike steps, and paused without bringing up his other foot. In vain Bull spoke to him, softly, steadily. Diablo took another step, quickened to a soft trot, and stopped suddenly. That weight on his back failed to leave him. He began to tremble violently. Bull felt the sudden thundering of the great heart beneath the pressure of his knee.

To the stallion, this man had been a friend, a constant companion. The touch of his hand was pleasant. Pleasanter still was the continual deep murmur of the voice, reassuring, telling him of a superior and guardian mind looking out for his interests. Now that hand was stroking his sleek neck and that voice was steadily in his ear. But the position was the most hated one. To be sure, there was no saddle, no cutting, binding cinch, no drag of cruel Spanish curb to control his head, no tearing spurs to threaten him. But his flanks twitched where the spurs had dug in many a time, and he panted, remembering the cinches. Those memories built up a panic. He became unsure. The voice reached him less distinctly. Moreover it was a strange time of the evening. The light of the day was nearly done; the moon was barely up, and all things were ghostly and unreal in that slant light.

Something of all that went through the mind of Diablo was understood by Bull Hunter. It was telegraphed to him by the twitching and vibration of great muscles, by the stiff arching of the neck, and the snorting breathing. But he was beginning to forget fear. The stallion danced lightly forward, and as the wind struck the face of Bull Hunter he suddenly rejoiced. This was what he had dreamed of, to be carried thus lightly, easily. The weight that had crushed other horses was nothing to Diablo. It made him feel buoyant. He became tinglingly alert. On the back of Diablo not a horse of the mountains could overtake him if he fled; and not a man of the mountains could escape him if he pursued on the back of the stallion.

That thought had hardly formed in his excited mind when Diablo sprang, cat-footed, to one side. It made Bull Hunter sway, and he naturally sought to preserve his balance by gripping the powerful barrel of the horse with his knees. But at the first touch of the knee Diablo went suddenly mad. Exactly what he did Bull Hunter never knew. Indeed, it seemed that Diablo left his feet, shot a dizzy height into the air, and at the crest of his rise did three or four things at once. At any rate, as the stallion landed, Bull pitched from the arched back and hurtled forward and to the right side. He landed heavily against the ground, his head striking a small rock; and he lay there a moment, stunned.

Far off he heard Tod shrilling at him: "Bull! Are you hurt?"

He gathered himself together and arose. "I'm all right. Stay where you are!"

"Don't try him again. He'll kill you, Bull!"

"Maybe. But I'm going to try."

Diablo stood on the far side of the corral in the moonlight a splendid figure with haughty tail and head. Inwardly he was trembling, enraged. He knew what would come. He had thrown men before, and usually he had tried to batter them to pieces after they fell. This man he had no desire to batter. There had been no saddle, no bridle, no spurs, no quirt—nevertheless, he must not be controlled by the hand of any man! But having thrown the fellow, now other men would run on him, swinging the accursed ropes over their heads, shouting, cursing at him in strident voices. Vitally he yearned to break through the bars of the corral and flee, but the bars were there and he must stay in the inclosure with this friendly enemy. It was not the prostrate man he feared so much as vengeance from other men, for that had always been the way.

But no one came. No shouts were heard except from the small, thin, familiar voice of Tod. And presently the giant arose from the ground where he had fallen and came toward him. Diablo flattened his ears expectantly. At the first throat-tearing curse he would charge. But no curse came. The man approached, as always, with extended hand, and the voice was the smooth, gentle murmur that carries peace into the shadowy mind of a horse.

Something relaxed in Diablo. If the man did not resent being thrown off—if that were a sort of game, as it were—why should he, Diablo, resent having the man on his back? The hand touched his nose gently; another hand was stroking his neck.

Presently he was led to the fence and again that heavy weight slid onto his back. He crouched again, with waves of blind panic surging up in him, but the panic did not master his sense this time, and as his brain cleared he began to discover that there was no urging, no will of another imposed upon him. He could walk where he pleased, following his own sweet will, or else he could stand still. It made no difference; but the soft-touching hand and the deep, quiet voice were assuring him that the man was glad to be up there on his back.

Diablo turned his head. One ear quivered and came forward tentatively; then the other. He had accepted Bull Hunter.

Afterward Bull found Tod. The boy wrung his hand ecstatically.

"That's what I call game!" he said.

"Why, Tod," the big man smiled, "you did the same thing."

"He knew I was nothing. But you're a growed man. But—what's this, Bull? Your back's all wet."

"It's nothing much," said Bull calmly. "When I fell, my head hit a stone. There's some things worth paying for, and Diablo's one of them."

Chapter Seventeen

Battle

The cut proved, as he had said, to be a small thing; but it turned out that Diablo was far from won. He was haltered and he would carry Bull bareback. The saddle was quite another affair. So Bull returned to the idea of the barley sack, with gradual additions. On each side of the sack he attached hanging straps. Diablo snorted at these and tried them with his teeth. They reminded him vaguely of the swinging stirrups that had so often battered his tender sides. He discovered that the straps were not alive, however, and were not harmful. And when their length was increased and an uncovered stirrup was tied on each side, he gradually became accustomed to these also. The next stage was passing the straps under his belly. They were tied there loosely, but the circle was completed, and Diablo, examining them critically, found nothing wrong. Then, a dozen times in a single evening, the straps were drawn up, tighter and tighter, until they touched him. At this he became excited, and it required all the resourcefulness of Bull to quiet him. But in three days the barley sack and its queer-looking additions had been changed for a true saddle—with the cinches drawn up tight enough for riding. And this without eliciting a single bucking spasm from Diablo!

Not even to Tod did Bull Hunter impart his great tidings. He had not yet climbed into that real saddle; Diablo had not yet heard the creak of the stirrup leathers under the weight of his rider. Indeed, there was still much to be done before the happy day when he saddled the black stallion and took down the bars of the corral gate and rode him out. And rode him without a bit! For on the point of steel in the mouth of Diablo, Bull Hunter knew that the horse would be against it resolutely. So he confined himself to a light hackamore alone. That was enough, for Diablo had learned to rein over the neck and stop at the slightest pull of the reins.

The next morning he went out to his work

with a light heart. They had had the help of several new men during the past ten days and now the frame of the roof was almost completed. It would not be long before Bull's services could be dispensed with and he connected the idea of the completion of the barn in a symbolic fashion with the completion of his conquest of the stallion. The two would be accomplished in the same moment, as it were. No wonder, then, that as he climbed the ladder up the side of the barn, with the ladder quaking beneath his weight, Bull Hunter began to sing, his thundering bass ringing among the ranch buildings until Mrs. Bridewell opened the kitchen window to hear the better, and old Bridewell stopped his ears in mock dismay at the thunder of Bull's voice.

But the work was not two hours old when little Tod scampered up to his side.

"Bull," he whispered, "Hal Dunbar is down yonder with a couple of men. He's come to ride Diablo. What'll we do, Bull? What'll we do?"

"Diablo will throw him," said Bull with conviction.

"But he won't. He can't," stammered the boy in his excitement. "Nothing could throw Hal Dunbar. Wait till you see him! Just you wait till you see. Gee, Bull, he's as big as you and—"

The other qualifications were apparently too amazing to be adequately described by the vocabulary of Tod.

"If any other man can ride Diablo," said Bull at length, "I don't think I care about him so much. I've been figuring that I'm the only man who can get on his back. If somebody else can handle him, they're welcome to the horse as far as I'm concerned."

"Are you going to let him go like that?" Tod was bitter with shame and anger. "After all our work, are you going to give him up without a fight?"

"A fight would be a gunfight, and a gunfight ends up in a death," said Bull gently. "I don't like bloodshed, Tod!"

The boy writhed. Here was an idol smashed with a vengeance!

"I might of knowed!" he groaned. "You ain't nothing but—but a big hulk!"

And he turned on his heel and gave the exciting news to his father.

For an event of this caliber, Bridewell called down all his men from the building, and they started for the corral. Hal Dunbar and his two men already were standing close to the bars, and Diablo stood quivering, high-headed, in the center of the inclosure. But, of the picture, the attention of Bull Hunter centered mainly on Hal Dunbar.

His dreams of the man had been true. He was a huge fellow, as tall as Bull, or taller, and nearly as bulky. But about Bull Hunter there

202

was a suggestion of ponderous unwieldiness, and there was none of that sugestion about Hal Dunbar. He was lithe and straight as a poplar, and as supple in his movements. The poise of his head and the alertness of his body and something of lightness in his whole posture told of the trained athlete. Providence had given the man a marvelous body, and he had improved it to the uttermost. To crown all, there was a remarkably handsome face, dark eyes and coal-black hair.

Yet, more than the imposing body of this hero of the ranges, Bull was impressed by the spirit of the man. The thing that Tod had felt, he felt in turn. It shone from the eye, it spoke in the set of Dunbar's mouth, something unconquerable. It was impossible, after a single glance, to imagine this man failing. Diablo, it was true, had the same invincible air. Indeed, they seemed meant for each other, this horse and this man. They might have been picked from a crowd and the one assigned to the other. Huge, lithe, fleet, powerful, and fiercely free, surely Hal Dunbar was intended by fate to sit in the saddle and govern Diablo according to his will.

The heart of Charlie Hunter sank. Here was the end, then, of all the love he had put into his work, of all the feminine gentleness with which he had petted Diablo and soothed him. And he discovered, in that bitter moment, that he had not worked merely to gain control of the horse. There would be no joy in making Diablo bend to his will. His aim was, and from the first unconsciously had been, to win Diablo so that the stallion would serve him joyously and freely out of the love he bore him. As he thought of this, his glance rested on the long, spoon-handled spurs of big Hal Dunbar.

Dunbar was shaking hands with Bridewell, leaning a trifle over the little old man.

"Here's one that'll be sorry to see you ride Diablo," said Bridewell. He pointed to Hunter. "He's been working weeks, trying to make a pet out of the hoss."

"A pet out of him? A pet?" echoed Dunbar.

He measured Bull Hunter with a certain bright interest. The sleeves of Bull were rolled up to the elbows and down the forearms ran the tangling masses of muscle. But the interest of Dunbar was only momentary. Presently his lip curled slightly, and he turned his haughty head toward the great stallion.

"I'll do something more than pet him. I'll make something useful out of the big brute. Saddle him, boys!"

He gestured carelessly, and his two attendants started toward the corral, one with a heavy saddle and one with a rope. As he stood rolling his cigarette and watching negligently, he impressed Bull as a veritable knight of the ranges, a baron with baronial adherents. It came partly from his splendid stature, and more from his flauntingly rich costume. The heavy gold braid on the sombrero, the gilded spurs, the brilliant silk shirt would have been out of place on another man, but they fitted in with Hal Dunbar. They were adjuncts to the pride of his face. Bull's attention wavered to Tod.

"Are—are they going to rope—Diablo?"

Tod flashed a half-disgusted, half-despairing glance up at his companion.

"What d'you think they're going to do? What do you think?"

Bull turned away, sick hearted. He could not bear the thought of the great stallion struggling helpless in the snaky coils of the rope. But of course there was no other way. Yet his muscles tightened, and the perspiration poured out on his forehead as he heard a shout from one of the men, then a brief drumming of Diablo's hoofs, and finally the heavy thud as the stallion struck full length on the ground.

That sound stunned Bull as though he had received a blow himself. Every nerve in him was tingling, revolting against the brutality. They were idiots, hopeless fools, to dream of conquering Diablo by brute force. And if they succeeded, they would have a broken-spirited horse on their hands, worse than useless, or else a treacherous man-killer to the end of his days.

He looked again. Diablo, saddled and blind-folded, was being driven out of the corral; a man held him on either side, and his mouth, dragged out, was already bleeding from the cruel Spanish bit. At that Bull Hunter saw red.

When his senses returned to him, he went hurriedly to Dunbar.

"Friend," he said, earnestly pleading, "will you let me make a suggestion?"

The insolent dark eyes ran over him mockingly.

"Oh, you're the fellow who tried to make a pet out of Diablo? Well, what's the suggestion?"

"If you wear those spurs you'll drive him mad! Take 'em off, Mr. Dunbar!"

Dunbar stared at him in amazement, and then looked to the others. "Did you hear that? This wise one wants me to try to ride without spurs. Who taught you to ride, eh?"

"I don't know much about it," confessed Bull humbly, "but I know you're apt to cut him up badly with those big spurs."

"And what the devil difference does that make to you?" cried Dunbar with heat. "And what do you mean by all these fool suggestions? I'm riding the horse!"

Bull drew back, downheaded. Hal Dunbar cast one contemptuous glance toward him and then stepped to the side of Diablo. The stallion was quivering and crouching with fear and anger, and shaking his head from time to time to get clear of the bandage which blinded him and made him helpless. Now and then he reared a little and came down on prancing forefeet, and Bull noted the spring and play of the fetlock joints. The whole running mechanism of the horse, indeed, seemed composed of coiled springs. Once released, what would the result be? And the first hope entered his mind, the first hope since he had seen the proud form of Hal Dunbar.

Now the big man set his hand on the pommel and vaulted into the saddle with a lightness that Bull admired hugely. Under the impact of that descending bulk the stallion crouched almost to the earth, but he came up again with a snort and a strangled neigh of rage.

"Are you ready?" called Dunbar, gathering the reins, and giving the string of his quirt another twist around his right hand.

One of his men had mounted his horse with a rope, the noose end of which was around Diablo's neck. This would serve as a pivot block to keep Diablo running in a circle. If he tried to run in a straight line the running noose would stop him and choke him down. He would have to gallop in a circle for his bucking, and to help keep him in that circle, the spectators now grouped themselves loosely in a wide rim. But

Bull Hunter did not move. From where he stood he could see all that he wished.

"All ready!" called the man with the rope.

"Let her go, then!"

The bandage was torn from the eyes of the stallion by Dunbar's second assistant, and the fellow leaped aside as he did so. Even then he barely escaped. Diablo had launched himself in pursuit, and his teeth snapped a fraction of an inch from the shoulder of the fugitive as the rope came taut and jerked him aside, and the full weight of Dunbar was thrown back on the reins.

That mighty wrench of back and shoulder and arm would have broken the jaw of an ordinary horse; it hardly disturbed Diablo. His head was first tucked back until his chin was against his breast, but a moment later he was head down, bucking as never horse bucked before. One second earlier Hal Dunbar had seemed almost as powerful as the animal he rode; now he suddenly became small.

For one thing Diablo wasted no time running against the rope. He followed the line of least resistance and bolted around the wide circle with tremendous leaps, gathering impetus as he ran—then stopping in midcareer by the terrific process of hurling himself in the air and coming down on four stiff legs and with his back humped so that the rider sat at the uneasy apex of a pyramid. And this was merely a beginning. That wild category of tricks which Bull had seen partially unraveled the first time he visited the horse was now brought forth again, enlarged, improved upon, made more intricate, intensified. But well and nobly did Hal Dunbar sustain his fame as a peerless rider. He rode straight up, and a cheer came from the spectators when they saw that he was not touching leather in the midst of the fiercest contortions of Diablo. It seemed that the great brute would snap the very saddle off his back, but still the rider sat erect, swaying as though in a storm, but still firmly glued to the saddle.

Even the heart of Bull Hunter warmed to the battle. They were a brutally glorious pair as they struggled. The wrenching hand of the rider and the Spanish bit had bloodied the mouth of the stallion, the spurs were clinging horribly at his sides, and he fought back like a mad thing. He flung himself on the ground, Dunbar barely slipping from the saddle in time, and whipped onto his feet again, but as he lurched up, he carried the weight of the rider again, for Dunbar had leaped into his seat, and as Diablo came up on all fours, it could be seen that the big man had secured both stirrups—the difficult thing in that feature of the fight. Dunbar urged the stallion on with a yell; and swinging the quirt over his head, he brought it down with a stinging cut on the silky flanks of the great horse. Bull Hunter crouched as though the lash had cut into his own flesh. He became savage for the moment. He wanted to have his hands on that rider!

But the cut of the quirt transformed Diablo. If he had fought hard before, he now fell into a truly demoniacal frenzy. The long flashing legs were springs indeed, and the moment his hoofs struck the earth he was flung up again to a greater height. He was sunfishing now in that most deadly manner when the horse lands on one forehoof, the rider receiving a double jar from the down-shock and then the whiplash snap to the side. Hal Dunbar was no longer using his quirt. It dangled idly at his side. The joy had gone from his face. In its place, as shock after shock benumbed his brain, there was an expression of fierce despair. Neither was he riding straight up, but he was pulling leather.

Otherwise, nothing human could have retained a seat in the saddle for an instant. Diablo, squealing, snorting, and grunting with effort, was dashing back and forth, flinging himself aloft, coming down on one stiff leg, doubling back with jackrabbit agility.

There was no longer applause from the onlookers. Old Bridewell himself in all of his years had never seen riding such as this, and it seemed that Diablo at last had met his master. Never had he fought as he fought now; never had he been stayed with as he was now. With foam and sweat the great black was reeking, but never once were the efforts relaxed. It was too terrible a sight to be applauded.

Then, at the end of a run, instead of hurling himself into the air as he had usually done before, Diablo flung himself down and rolled. It caught Dunbar by surprise, but the yell of horror from the bystanders stimulated him to sharp action, and he was out of the saddle in the last hair's breadth of time.

Diablo had been carried on over to his feet by the impetus of the fall, and he was already rising when Dunbar leaped for the saddle. Fair and true he struck the saddle and with marvelous skill his left foot caught the stirrup and clung to it—but the right foot missed its aim, and, before Dunbar could lodge his foot squarely, the stirrup was dancing crazily as Diablo began a wild combination of cross-bucking and sunfishing. The hat snapped from the head of Dunbar and his long black hair tossed; with both hands he was clinging. All joy of battle was gone from him. In its place was staring fear, for his right foot was still out of the stirrup.

"Choke him down! Choke him—" he shrieked.

Before he could be obeyed by his confused henchmen, Diablo shot into the air and at the very crest of his rise, bucked. Dunbar lurched to one side. There was a groan from the by-standers; and the next instant the stallion, land-ing on the one stiffened foreleg, had snapped his rider from the saddle and hurled him to the ground.

He lay in a shapeless heap, and the stallion whirled to finish his enemy.

Chapter Eighteen

New Fields Ahead

Every second of the fight Bull Hunter had followed the actions of the horse as though he were directing them from the distance with some electric form of communication and control. When Hal Dunbar with a yell of despair was flung sidewise in the saddle as Diablo bucked in midair, Bull Hunter knew what was coming and lurched through the line of watchers. Straight across the open space of the circle he raced as he had never run before, and while the others stood frozen, while the man with the rope tugged futilely, Bull came in front of the stallion as Diablo whirled to smash his late rider to a pulp. There was no question of Dunbar crawling out of the way. He had rolled on his back with arms outstretched, helplessly stunned. Even in the lightning speed of the action Bull found time to wonder what would be the result if the hoof of the wild horse crashed down into that upturned, handsome face, now stained with crimson and black with dust.

He had no time to imagine further. Diablo, red-eyed with anger, had whirled on him and reared, and swerving from those terrible, pawing hoofs, Bull Hunter leaped in and up. His goal was not the tossing bridle rein, but the stout strap which circled the head just above the bit, and his big right hand jarred home on this goal. All his weight was behind his stiffened arm, and under the blow the stallion lurched higher. A down-sweep of a forefoot gashed Bull's shoulder and tore his shirt to shreds. But he pressed, expecting every instant the finishing blow on his head. In he went, with all his weight behind the effort, and felt the stallion stagger on his hind legs, then topple, lose balance, and fall with a crash on his side!

Bull followed him in the fall, for half a step, then whirled, scooped the nerveless body of Hal Dunbar in his arms, and rushed staggering under the burden to the edge of the circle. Diablo had regained his footing instantly, but as he strove to follow, the rope had drawn taut about his throat, and he was checked.

As for Bull Hunter, he laid the senseless burden down in safety, and turned toward the stallion. One haunting fear was in his mind. Had Diablo been sufficiently blinded in the excitement of the battle to fail to recognize him, or had the great horse known the hand that toppled it back? In the latter case Bull Hunter could never come near the black without peril of his life.

In a gloomy quandary he stared at the trembling, shining giant, who stood with his head high and his tail flaunting, and all the fierce pride of victory in his eye. One knot of people had gathered over the fallen Hal Dunbar, but some remained, dazed and gaping, looking at the form of the conqueror. A wild temptation came to Bull to test the horse even in this crisis of excitement, with every evil passion roused in him. He stepped out again, his right hand extended, his voice soft.

"Diablo!"

The stallion jerked his head toward the voice, but the head was twitched away as the man with the rope brought it taut again.

"You fool!" he shouted. "Get back, or the hoss'll nail you!"

Unreasoning rage poured thrilling through Bull Hunter. He shook his great fist at the other.

"Slack away on that rope or I'll break you in two!"

There was a moment of amazed silence; then, with a curse, the rider threw the rope on the ground.

"Get your head broke then!"

Bull Hunter had forgotten him already. He had resumed that approach. At his voice the stallion turned that proud and terrible head—with the ears flattened against his neck. It gave him an ominous, snakelike appearance about the head, but still Bull went steadily and slowly toward him with his hand out, that ancient gesture of peace and good will. There were shouts and warnings from the others. Hal Dunbar, his senses returned, had staggered to his feet; he had received no injury in the fall, and now he gaped in amazement at this empty-handed man approaching the stallion. And Diablo was no longer controlled by the rope!

But all the outcries meant nothing to Bull Hunter. They faded to a blur. All he saw was the head of the stallion. Had he known and remembered that fall and the hand that forced him to it? He could not tell. There might be any murderous intent in that quivering, crouching form.

Just that name, over and over again, very softly: "Diablo! Steady, Diablo!"

Now he was within two paces—in a yard—his fingers were close to the terrible head—and the ears of Diablo pricked forward.

"Ah, Diablo! They'll never touch you with the spurs again!"

The stallion made a long step, and with his head raised he looked over the shoulder of Bull Hunter and snorted his defiance at all other men in the world! And down his neck the big, gentle hand was running, soothing his quivering body, and the steady voice was bringing infinite messages of reassurance to the troubled brain. That hand was loosening now the rope which was burning into his neck—loosening it, drawing it off. And now the bridle followed; and Diablo's mouth was free from the cruel taint of the steel. The head of the stallion turned—great, soft eyes looked into the face of Bull Hunter and accepted him as a friend forever.

Hal Dunbar, groggy from the shock of the fall, staggered toward them.

"Get away from that horse!" he commanded. "Hey, Riley, grab Diablo for me again. I'll ride him this time."

He was too unsteady to walk in a straight line, but the fire of battle was in his eyes again. There was no doubting the gameness of the big man. Old Bridewell caught his arm and drew him back.

"If Diablo gets a sniff of you on the wind he'll come at you like a wolf. Stand back here—and watch!"

Hal Dunbar was too dazed to resist. Besides, he began to see that all eyes were focused on the black stallion and the man beside him. That man was the huge, cloddish stranger who had advised him to ride without spurs. Then the full meaning came to Dunbar. The rope was no longer around the neck of the stallion. The very bridle had been taken from his head, and yet the stranger stood undaunted beside him, and the stallion did not seem to be angered by that nearness.

The next thing Dunbar heard was the voice of Bridewell saying: "Nerviest thing I ever seen. I been putting this Bull Hunter down for a half-wit, pretty near. All his strength in his back and none in his head. But I changed my mind to-day. When you hit the ground, Diablo whirled on you, and he'd of smashed you to bits before they could choke him down and pull him away, but Bull came out of the crowd on the run, grabbed the bridle, made Diablo rear, took that cut on his shoulder, and threw him fair and square. Finest, coolest, headiest thing I ever seen done with a hoss in a pinch. And he saved your skin, Dunbar. You'd be a mess this minute, if it wasn't for Hunter! He threw Diablo and turned around and picked you up as if you was a baby and packed you over here. Then he went back—and you see what's he's doing?"

"He saved my life?" muttered Dunbar. "That big—he saved my life?"

Gratitude, for the moment at least, was obscured in his mind. All he felt vividly was a burning shame. He, Hal Dunbar, the invincible, had been beaten fairly and squarely in the battle with the horse; not only this, he had been saved from complete destruction only by the intervention of this nonentity, this Bull Hunter whom he had scorned only a few moments before. He looked about him in blind anger at the bystanders. Worst of all, this was a new country where he was only vaguely known, and whenever his name was mentioned in these parts in the future, there would be some one to tell of the superior prowess of Hunter, and how the life of Dunbar was thrown away and saved by another. No wonder that big Hal Dunbar writhed with the shame of it.

He forgot even that emotion now in wonder at what was happening. Hunter had stepped to the side of the horse, raised his foot, and put it in the stirrup. Did the fool intend to climb into the saddle while that black devil was not blindfolded, without even a bridle?

That, in fact, was what he was doing. The steady murmur of the voice of Hunter reached him as the big man soothed the horse. He saw the head of Diablo turn, saw him sniff the shoulder of his companion, and then Hunter lifted himself slowly into the saddle. There was a groan of excitement from the spectators, and at the sound rather than at the weight on his back, Diablo crouched. It was only for a moment that he quivered, wild-eyed, irresolute. Then he straightened and threw up his head. Bull Hunter, his face white and drawn, but his mouth resolute, had touched the shining flank of the stallion, and Diablo moved into a soft trot, gentle as the flowing of water.

Before him the circle split and rolled back. He glided through, guided by a hand that touched lightly on his neck, and in an utter silence he was seen to turn the corner of the nearest shed and approach the corral. Hal Dunbar, rubbing his eyes, was the first to speak.

"A trick horse!" he said. "By the Lord, a trick horse!"

"The first time I ever seen him play that trick," gasped old Bridewell, his eyes huge and round, "except when Tod was up on him. I dunno what's happened. It's like a dream. But there's a saddle on him now, and that was something even Tod could never make him stand. I dunno what's happened!"

The little crowd broke up into chattering groups. Here had been a thing that would bear telling and retelling for many a year. In the confusion Dunbar's man, Riley, approached his employer.

Both gratitude and shame were forgotten by Dunbar now. He gripped the shoulder of this man and groaned: "I've lost him, Riley! The only horse ever foaled that could have carried me the way a man should be carried. Now I'll have to ride plow horses the rest of my life!"

He pointed to the cloddish, heavy-limbed gray which he had ridden in his quest for the super-horse at the Bridewell place.

"I been thinking," said Riley. "I been thinking a pile the last few minutes."

"What you been thinking about? What good does thinking do me? I've lost the horse, haven't I, and that half-wit has him?"

"He has him—now," suggested Riley, watching the face of the big man for fear that he might go too far.

"You mean by that?" queried the master.

"Exactly," said Riley. "Because he has the black now, it doesn't mean that he's going to have him forever, does it?"

"Riley, you're a devil. That fellow saved my life, they tell me."

"I don't mean you're going to bump him off. But suppose you get him to come and work on your place? There might be ways of getting the hoss—buying him or something. Get him there, and we'll find a way. Besides, he can teach you how to handle the hoss before you get him. I say it's all turned out for the best."

221

Dunbar frowned. "Take him with me? And every place I go hear it said: 'There's the man who rode the horse that threw Dunbar!' No, curse him, I'll see him in Hades before I take him with me!"

"How else are you going to get the hoss? Tell me that?"

"That's it," muttered Dunbar. "I've got to have him. I've got to have him! Did you watch? I felt as if the big black devil had wings."

"He had you in the air most of the time, all right," and Riley grinned.

"Shut up," snapped his master. "But the chief thing is, I want to show that big black fiend that I'm his master. He—he's beaten me once. But one beating doesn't finish me!"

"Then go get Hunter to come with us when we ride back."

Dunbar hesitated another instant and then nodded. "It has to be done."

He strode off in pursuit of Bull and presently found the big man in the corral rubbing down the stallion; the little bright-eyed Tod was close beside them. It had been a great day for Tod. First he had felt that his giant pupil was disgraced—a man without spirit. And then, in the time of blackest doubt, Bull Hunter had become a hero and accomplished the great feat—ridden Diablo, before all the incredulous eyes of the watchers. All of Tod's own efforts had been repaid a thousandfold when he heard Bull say to one of those who followed with questions and admiration: "It's not my work. Tod showed me how to go about it. Tod deserves the credit."

That was the reason that Tod's eyes now were supernally bright when big Hal Dunbar approached. Diablo showed signs of excitement, but Charlie Hunter quieted him with a word and went to the bars of the corral. The hand of Dunbar was stretched out, and Bull took it with humble earnestness.

"I'm glad you weren't hurt bad," he said. "For a minute or two I was scared that Diablo—"

"I know," cut in Dunbar, for he detested a new description of the scene of his failure. Then he made himself smile. "But I've come to thank you for what you did, Hunter. Between you and me, I know that I talked rather sharp to you a while back. I'm sorry for that. And now—why, man, your side must be wounded!"

"It's just a little scratch," said Bull goodnaturedly. "It isn't the first time that Diablo has made me bleed but now—well, isn't he worth a fight, Mr. Dunbar?"

And he gestured to the magnificent, watchful head of the stallion. The heart of Hal Dunbar swelled in him. By fair means or foul, he must have that horse, and on the spot he made his proposition to Hunter. He had only to climb on the back of Diablo and ride south with him; the pay would be anything—double what he got from Bridewell, who, besides, was almost through with him, Dunbar understood.

"But I'm not much good," and Bull sighed reluctantly. "I can't use a rope, and I don't know cattle, and—"

"I'll find uses for you. Will you come?"

So it was settled. But before Bull climbed into the saddle and started off after Dunbar, little Tod drew him to one side.

"There ain't any good in Dunbar. Watch him and—remember me, Bull."

Chapter Nineteen

The Girl in the Case

That ride to the southern mountains seemed to Bull Hunter to mark a great point of departure between his old life and a new life.

He had not heard Riley, fox-faced and wicked of eye, say to his master: "What this big fool needs is a little kidding. Make him think that we figure him to be a big gun." He had not seen Hal Dunbar make a wry face before he nodded.

All that Bull Hunter could know was that the three men, Riley, Dunbar, and Joe Castor, were all exceedingly pleasant to him on the way. Of all the men in the world, only Pete Reeve, had treated him as these men were now doing, and it was sweet beyond measure to Bull Hunter to be treated with considerate respect, to have his opinion asked, to be deferred to and flattered. As for the thousand little asides with which they made a mock of him, they were far above his head. It seemed only patent to Bull Hunter that he had been accepted freely into the equal society of men.

He drew a vague comparison between that success and his mastery of Diablo. The big stallion was like a kitten under his hand. It required much coaxing during the first half day of riding to bring Diablo within speaking distance of the other men, but gradually he discovered that they could do him no harm so long as the gentle voice of Hunter was near him; thereafter he was entirely amenable to reason. One could see that the stallion was learning difficult lessons, but he was learning them fast. Eye and ear and scent told him that these creatures were dangerous. Old experience told him that they were dangerous, and only a blind trust in Bull Hunter enabled him to conquer the panic which surged up in his brain time and again. But he kept on trying, and the constant struggle against men, which had featured his life, made him astonishingly quick to pick up new facts. The first step had been the hard one, and it seemed to Bull Hunter that the closeknit, smooth-flowing muscles beneath him were carrying him onward into the esteem of all men. To Diablo he gave the praise, and after Diablo to little freckled Tod, and to Pete Reeve, the fighter. As for taking any credit to himself, that idea never came to him for a moment.

The long trip took two days. They crossed the green, rolling hills; they passed the foothills, and climbing steadily they came onto a broad, high plateau—it was a natural kingdom, this ranch of the Dunbars. The fence around it was the continuous range of mountains skirting the plateau on all sides, and in every direction up to those blue summits as far as the eye carried, stretched the land which owned Hal Dunbar as master. To Bull Hunter, when they reached the crest, and the broad domain was pointed out to him, this seemed a princely stretch indeed, and Hal Dunbar was more like a king than ever. It was easy to forgive pride in such a man and a certain asperity of temper. How could so rich and powerful a man be like others?

The ranch house was worthy of such a holding. A heavy growth of beautiful silver spruce swept up the slope of some hills, and riding through the forest, one caught the first glimpse of the building. It was spread out carelessly, the foundations laid deep to cover the irregularities of the ground. It was a heterogeneous mass, obviously not the work of any one builder. Here a one-story wing rambled far to the side, built heavily, of logs rudely squared, and there was a three-story frame section of the house; and still again there was a tall tower effect of rough stone. As for the barns and sheds which swept away down the farther and lower slopes, the meanest of them looked to Bull as though it might have made a home of more than average comfort.

The three other riders noted the gaping astonishment of Bull and passed the wink quietly around. To Hal Dunbar it was growing more and more annoying that he had to trouble himself with such a clod of a man and use diplomacy where contemptuous force would have been so much more after his heart. But he continued to follow the scheme first laid down for his pursuit by clever Riley, and when they came to the wide-ranging stable he assigned the black stallion to a roomy box stall. Bull Hunter thanked him for the courtesy as though it had been a direct personal favor; as a matter of fact, Hal felt that he was merely taking care of a horse which was already as good as his.

Coming back toward the house Bull walked slowly in the rear of the little party. He wanted to take plenty of time and drink in the astonishing details of what to him was a palace. And about the weather-beaten old house he felt that there was a touch of mystery of a more or less feudal romance. Climbing the steps to the porch he turned; a broad sweep of hills opened above the tops of the spruces, and the blue mountains were piled beyond.

While he stood, a door slammed, and he heard a mellow girl's voice calling: "Hello, Hal, what luck?"

"What luck? No luck!" grumbled young Dunbar. "All the luck has gone the way of my—friend—here." He brought out the last words joltingly. "This is Charlie Hunter, commonly called Bull for reasons you may guess. Bull, this is Mary Hood."

Bull had turned lumberingly, and he found himself staring at a girl in a more formal riding outfit than he had ever seen before, with tall boots of soft red leather, and a little round black hat set on her hair, and a coat fitted somewhat closely. The rather masculine outfit only served to make her freer, more independent, more delightfully herself, Bull Hunter thought. She looked him up and down and reserved judgment, it seemed.

"He rode Diablo," Dunbar was explaining.

"And that's why you brought him?" she asked, flashing a queer glance at Hal.

Then she came a pace down the steps and shook hands with Bull. He took the small hand carefully, with a fear that the bones would break unless he were excessively gentle. At that she laughed so frankly that a tingle went through his big body, and he peered closely at her. As a rule the laughter of others made him hot with shame, but this laughter was different; it seemed to invite him into a pleasant secret.

"I'm glad to meet the man who conquered Diablo," she was saying.

"I didn't beat Diablo," he hastened to explain. "We just sort of reached an understanding. He saw that I didn't mean him any harm—so he let me ride him. That's all there was to it!"

He saw her eyes narrow a trifle as she looked down at him, for she had drawn back to the level of the porch. Was she despising him and condemning him merely because he had told her the truth? He flushed at the thought, and then he was called into the house by Dunbar and brought to a room. The size of it inspired him with a profound awe, and he was still gaping when Dunbar left him.

In the hall the master of the house met Riley, and the fox-faced lieutenant drew him aside.

"I've got a plan," he said.

"You're full of plans," muttered Dunbar evilly.

All the way home he had been striving to find some way of explaining his lack of success with the stallion to Mary Hood. She had grown up on the ranch with him, for her father had been the manager of the ranch for twenty years; and she had grown up with the feeling that Hal Dunbar was infallible and invincible.

"Did you see the big hulk look at Mary Hood?" Riley asked.

That name came pat with the unpleasant part of Hal's brooding, and his scowl grew blacker. "What about it?"

"Looked at her as though she was an angel—touched her hand as though it was fire. I tell you, Hal, she knocked Hunter clean off his balance."

"Not the first she's done that to," said Hal with meaning.

"Maybe not. Maybe not," said Riley rather hastily. "But I been thinking. Suppose you go to Mary and tell her that you're dead set on keeping this Hunter with you. Tell her that he's a hard fellow to handle, that he likes her, and that the best way to make sure of him is for her to be nice to him. She can do that easy. She takes nacheral to flirting."

"Flirt with that thick-head? She'd laugh in my face."

"She'd do more than that for you, Hal."

"H'm," grunted Dunbar, greatly mollified. "I ask her to make Hunter happy. What comes of it? If her father sees Hunter make eyes at her he'll blow the head off the clodhopper."

"I know." Riley nodded. "He's always afraid she'll take a fancy to one of the hands and run off with him, or something like that. He's dead set agin' her saying two words to anybody like me, say!"

He gritted his teeth and flushed at the thought. Then he continued: "But that's just what you want. You want to get Hunter's head blown off, don't you?"

Dunbar caught the shoulder of Riley and whirled him around.

"Are you talking murder to me, Riley?"

"I'm talking sense," said Riley.

"By the Lord," growled Dunbar, "you're a plain bad one, Riley. You like deviltry for the sake of the deviltry itself. You want me to get—"

"How much do you want the black hoss, chief?"

Dunbar sighed.

"You can't touch him, after him saving your life, and I can't touch him, because everybody knows that I'm your man. But suppose you get the girl and Hunter planted? Then when Jack Hood rides in this afternoon, I'll take him where he can see 'em together. Leave the rest to me. Will you? I'll have Jack Hood scared she's going to elope before morning, and Jack will do the rest. You know his way."

"Suppose Hood gets killed?"

"Killed—by that? Jack Hood? Why, you know he's near as good as you with his gat!"

Dunbar nodded slowly. After all, the scheme was a simple one.

"Well?" whispered Riley.

"You and the devil win," said Hal. "After all, what's this Hunter amount to? Nothing. And I need the horse!"

He executed the first step of the scheme instantly. He went downstairs and found the girl still on the veranda. She began to mock him at once.

"You'll go to heaven, Hal, giving a home to the man who beats you."

He managed to smile, although the words were poison to him. He had loved her as long as he could remember, and soon or later she would be his wife, but the period remained indefinitely in the future as the whims of the girl changed. It was for that reason, as Hal very well knew, that her father became furious when she smiled at another man. The rich marriage was his goal; and when a second man stepped onto the stage, old Jack Hood was ready to fight. Hal saw a way of stopping her gibes and proving his good intentions toward Hunter all in a breath.

"He saved my life, Mary. I lost a stirrup, and the devil of a horse threw me."

Briefly he sketched in the story of the rescue, and how Bull Hunter afterward had ridden the horse without spurs, without a bridle. Before he ended her eyes were shining.

"That's what he meant when he said that he hadn't beaten Diablo. I understand now. At the time I thought he was a little simple, Hal."

"He's not exceptionally clever, Mary," said Hal, "and that's where the point comes in of what I want you to do. Hunter is apt to take a fancy that he isn't wanted here—that he's being kept out of charity because he saved my life. Nothing I can say will convince him. I want you to give him a better reason for staying around. Will you do it—as a great favor?"

She dropped her chin into her hand and studied him.

"Just what are you driving at, Hal?"

"You know what I mean well enough. I want you to waste a smile or two on him, Mary. Will you do that? Make him think you like him a good deal, that you're glad to have him around. Will you? Take him out for a walk this afternoon and get him to tell you the story of his life. You can always make a man talk and generally you turn them into fools. You've done it with me, often enough," he added gloomily.

"Flirt with that big, quiet fellow?" she said gravely. "Hal, you're criminal. Besides, you know that I don't flirt. It's just the opposite. When I like a man I'm simply frank about it."

"But you have a way of being frank so that a poor devil usually thinks you want to marry him, and then there's the devil to pay. You know it perfectly well."

"That's not true, Hal!"

"I won't argue. But will you do it?"

"Absolutely not!"

"It might be quite a game. He may not be altogether a fool. And suppose he were to wake up? Suppose he's simply half asleep?"

He saw a gleam of excitement come in her eyes and wisely left her without another word. After things had reached a certain point Mary could be generally trusted to carry the action on.

Chapter Twenty

The Unexpected

Jack Hood had ridden out on his rounds with a new horse that morning, and the new horse developed the gait of a plow horse. The result was that grim old Jack reached the house that night with a body racked by the labor of the day and a disposition poisoned for the entire evening. He was met at the stable by Riley, and the sight of him brought a spark for the moment into the eye of the foreman.

"You're back, then, and you got Diablo?"

"Look yonder."

Jack Hood went to the box stall and came back rubbing his hands, but his exultation was cut short by Riley's remark: "He doesn't belong to Hal. Hal was thrown and another gent rode him."

The amazement of Jack Hood took the shape of a wild torrent of profanity. He was proud of the ranch which he had controlled for so long, and still prouder of his young master. His creed included two main points—the essential beauty of his daughter and the infallibility of young Hal Dunbar; consequently his great ambition was to unite the two.

"Mary took to Hunter pretty kindly," concluded Riley, as they walked back toward the house at the conclusion of the story.

The foreman took off his hat and shook back his long, iron-gray hair.

"Trust her for that. Something new is always what she wants."

"They've got the new well pretty near sunk," said Riley. "Take a look at it?"

"All right."

But before they had gone halfway down the path onto which Riley had cunningly diverted the older man, he caught Hood's arm and stopped him with a whisper.

"Look at that. *Already!* This Hunter ain't such a slow worker, eh, Jack?"

They had come in view of the little terraced garden which was Mary's particular property; it was screened from the house by a rank or two of the spruce, and on a rustic bench, seated with their backs to the witnesses, were Mary and Bull Hunter. The girl was rapt in attention, and her eyes never left the face of Hunter. As for Bull, he was talking steadily, and it seemed to Jack Hood that as the big stranger talked he leaned closer and closer to the girl. The hint which Riley had already dropped was enough to inflame the imagination of the suspicious foreman; what he now saw was totally conclusive, he thought. Now, under his very eyes, he saw the big man stretch out his hand, and he saw the hand of Mary dropped into it.

It was more than Riley had dared to hope for. He caught Jack Hood by the shoulders, whirled him around, and half dragged him back to the house.

"Not in front of your daughter, Jack," he pleaded. "I don't blame you for being mad when a skunk like that starts flirting with a girl the first day he's seen her. But if you got anything to say to him, wait till Mary is out of the way. There goes the supper bell. Hurry on in. Keep hold on yourself."

"Do I have to sit through supper and look at that hound?"

"Not at all," suggested the cunning Riley. "Have a bite in the kitchen and go up to your room. I'll say that you got some figures to run over. Afterward, you can come down and jump him!"

He watched Jack Hood disappear, grinning faintly, and then hunted for Hal Dunbar.

"It's started," he said. "I dropped a word in Jack's ear and then showed him the two of 'em sitting together. It was like a spark in the powder. The old boy exploded."

"How close were they sitting?" asked Hal suspiciously.

"Close enough." Riley grinned, for he was not averse to making even Dunbar himself writhe.

The result was that Hal maneuvered to draw Mary Hood aside when she came in with big Hunter for supper. Something in Bull Hunter's face disturbed the owner of the ranch, for the eyes of Bull were alight, and he was smiling for no apparent reason.

"How did things go?" he asked carelessly.

"You were all wrong about him," said the girl earnestly. "He's not a half-wit by any means, Hal. I had a hard time of it at first, but then I got him talking about Diablo and the trouble ended. Not a bit of sentiment in him; but just like a great big, simple, honest boy, with a man's strength. It would have done you good to hear him!"

"And he'll stay with us?" asked Hal dryly, for he was far from enthusiastic.

"Of course he'll stay. Do you know what he

did? He promised to try to teach me to ride Diablo, and he even shook hands on it! Hal, I like him immensely!"

All during the meal the glances of Hal Dunbar alternated between the girl and the giant. He was more disturbed than he dared confess even to himself. It was not so much that Bull Hunter sat with a faintly dreamy smile, staring into the future and forgetting his food, but it was the fact that Mary Hood was continually smiling across the table into that big, calm face. Dunbar began to feel that the devil was indeed behind the wit of Riley.

He began to wait nervously for the coming of the girl's father and the explosion. As soon as supper was over, following the time-honored custom which the first Dunbar had established on the ranch, Mary left the room, and the men gathered in groups for cards or dice or talk, for they were not ordinary hired hands, but picked men. Many of them had grown gray in the Dunbar service. Now was the time for the coming of Jack Hood, and Hal had not long to wait.

The door at the far side of the big room was thrown open not five minutes after the disappearance of Mary Hood, and her father entered. He came with a brow as black as night, tossed a sharp word here and there in reply to the greetings, and going to the fireplace leaned against the mantel and rolled a cigarette. While he smoked, from under his shaggy brows he looked over the company.

Hal Dunbar waited, holding his breath. One brilliant picture was dawning on his mind—himself mounted on great black Diablo and swinging over the hills at a matchless gallop.

The picture vanished. Jack Hood had left the fireplace and was crossing the room with his alert, quick step. His nerves showed in that step; and it was nerve power that made him a dreaded gunfighter. His gloom seemed to have vanished now. He smiled here; he paused there for a cheery word; and so he came to where Bull Hunter sat with his long legs stretched before him and the unchanging, dreamy smile on his face.

Over those long legs Jack Hood stumbled. When he whirled on the seated man his cheer was gone and a devil was in his face.

"You damned lummox," he said, "what d'ye mean by tripping me?"

"Me?" gasped Bull, the smile gradually fading and blank amazement taking its place.

It was at this moment that a man stepped out of the shadow of the kitchen doorway, a very small, withered man. No doubt he was some late arrival asking hospitality for the night; and having come after supper was over, he had been fed in the kitchen and then sent in among the other men; for no one was turned away hungry

241

from the Dunbar house. He was so small, so light-footed, that he would hardly have been noticed at any time, and now that the roar from Jack Hood had focused all eyes on Bull Hunter, the newcomer was entirely overlooked. He seemed to make it a point to withdraw himself farther, for now he stepped into a dense shadow near the wall where he could see and remain unseen.

Jack Hood had shaken his fist under the nose of the seated giant.

"I mean it," he cried. "You tripped me, you skunk, and Jack Hood ain't old enough to take that from no man!"

Bull Hunter cast out deprecatory hands. The words of this fire-eyed fellow were bad enough, but the tigerish tenseness of his muscles was still worse. It meant battle, and the long, black-leather holster at the thigh of Hood meant battle of only one kind. It had come so suddenly on him that Bull Hunter was dazed.

"I'm sorry," he said. "I sure didn't mean to trip you—but maybe my foot might of slipped out a little and—"

"Slipped out!" sneered Hood. He stopped, panting with fury. That a comparative stranger should have dared to speak familiarly with his daughter was bad enough; that a blank-faced coward should have dared flirt with her, dared take her hand, was maddening.

"You infernal sneak!" he growled. "Are you going to try to get out of it, now that you've seen you can't bluff me down—that I won't stand for your tricks?"

Bull Hunter rose, slowly, unfolding his great bulk until he towered above the other; and yet the condensed activity of Hood was fully as formidable. There were pantherlike suggestions of speed about the arm that dangled beside his holster.

The withered little man in the shadow by the kitchen door took one noiseless step into the light—and then shrank back as though he had changed his mind.

"It looks to me," said Bull Hunter mildly, "that you're trying to force a fight on me. Stranger, I can't fight a man as old as you are."

Perhaps it was a tactless speech, but Bull was too dazed to think of grace in words. It brought a murderous snarl from the other.

"I'm old enough to be Jack Hood—maybe you've heard of me? And I'm young enough to polish off every unlicked cub in these parts. Now, curse you, what d'ye say to that?"

"I can only say," said Bull miserably, feeling his way, "that I don't want to fight."

With an oath Hood exclaimed: "A coward! They're all like that—every one of the big fellers. A yaller-hearted sneak!"

"Easy, Jack!" broke in one of the men.

"Let Jack alone," called the commanding voice of Hal Dunbar. "I saw Hunter trip him!"

"But," pleaded Bull Hunter, "I give you my word—"

"Shut up! I've heard enough of your talk."

Bull Hunter obediently stopped his talk.

A sickening quiet drew through the room. Men bowed their heads or turned them away, for such cowardice was not pleasant to see. The little man in the shadow raised one hand and brushed it across his face.

"I'll let you off one way," said Jack Hood. "Stand up here, and face the crowd and tell 'em you're a liar, that you're sorry for what you done!"

Bull faced the crowd. A shudder of expectancy went through them, and then they saw that his face was working, not with shame or fear but with a mental struggle, and then he spoke.

"Gents, it seems like I may be wrong. I may have tripped him, which I didn't meant to. But not knowing that I tripped him, I got to say that I can't call myself a liar. I can't apologize."

They were shocked into a new attention; they saw him turn and face the frown of Jack Hood.

"You're forcing this fight, stranger. And—if you keep on, you'll drop, sir. I promise you that!"

The sudden change in affairs had astonished

Jack Hood; now his astonishment gave way to a sort of hungry joy.

"I never was strong on words. I got two ways of talking and here's the one I like best!" As he uttered the last word he reached for his gun.

The little man glided out of the shadow, crouched, intense. It seemed to him that the hand of Bull Hunter hung moveless at his side while the gun flashed out from Hood's holster. He groaned at the thought, but in the last second, there was a move of Hunter's hand that no eye could follow, that singular convulsive twitch which Pete Reeve had taught him so long before. Only one gun spoke. Jack Hood spun sidewise and crashed to the floor, and his gun rattled far away.

By the time the first man had rushed to the fallen figure, the gun was back in Bull's holster.

The little man in the shadow heard him saying: "Pardners, he's not dead. He's shot through the right shoulder, low, beneath the joint. That bullet won't kill him, but get him bandaged quick!"

A calm, clear voice, it rang through the room. The little man slipped back into his shadow and straightened against the wall.

"He's right," said Hal Dunbar, stepping back from the cluster. "Riley and Jerry, get him up to his room and bandage him, quick! The rest of you stay here. We got a job. Hood's gun hung in the holster, and this fellow shot him down. A murdering, cowardly thing to do. You hear? A murdering, cowardly thing to do!"

Obviously he was wrong, and obviously not one of his henchmen would tell him so. For some reason the boss intended to take up the lost battle of Jack Hood. Why, was not theirs to reason, though plainly the fight had been fair, and Hood had been in the wrong from the first. They shifted swiftly, a man to each door, the others along the wall with their hands on their weapons. There was a change in big Bull Hunter. One long leap backward carried him into a corner of the room. He stood erect, and they could see his eyes gleaming in the shadow.

"I think you got me here to trap me, Dunbar," he called in such a voice that the little man in the shadow thrilled at the sound of it, "but you'll find that you're trapped first, my friend. Touch that gun of yours, and you're a dead man, Dunbar. Curse you, I dare you to go for it!"

Could this be Bull Hunter speaking? The little man in the shadow thrilled with joyous amazement.

Hal Dunbar evidently was going to fight the thing through. He stood swaying a little from side to side. "No guns out, boys, as yet. Wait till I take my crack at him, and then—"

The little man in the shadow stepped out into

the light and walked calmly toward the center of the room.

"Just a little wee minute, Dunbar," he was saying. "Just a little wee minute, Mr. Mantrapper Dunbar! I got a word to say."

"Who the devil are you?" cried Hal Dunbar, turning on this puny stranger.

A joyous shout from Bull Hunter drowned the answer of the other.

"Pete! Pete Reeve!"

The little man waved his hand carelessly to the giant in the corner.

"You give me a hard trail, Bull, old boy. But you didn't think you could slip me, did you? Not much. And here I am, pretty pronto on the dot, I figure." He took in with a glance the men along the walls. "You know me, boys, and I'm here to see fair play. They ain't going to be fair play in this room with you boys lined up waiting to drop Bull in case he plugs Dunbar. Dunbar, I know you. And between you and me, I don't know no good of you. You're young, but you're going to show later on. If you want to talk business to Bull Hunter some other time, you're welcome to come finding him, and he won't be hard to find. Bull, come along with me. Just back up, if you don't mind, Bull. Because they's murder in our friend Dunbar's face. And here we are!"

Side by side they drew back to the outer door

with big Hal Dunbar watching them from under a scowl, with never a word, and so through the door and into the night.

Two minutes later Diablo was rocking across the hills with his mighty stride, and the cow pony of Pete Reeve was pattering beside him.

As they drove through the great spruces, the moon rose. Bull Hunter greeted it with a thundering song and threw up his hand to it.

Pete Reeve swore softly in amazement and drew his horse to a walk.

"By the Lord," cried Bull, "and I haven't thanked you yet for pulling me out of that mess. I'd be crow's food by this time if it hadn't been for you, Pete!"

"That only wipes out one score. Let's talk about you, Bull. Since I last seen you, you've got to be a man. Was it dropping Hood that made you buck up like this?"

"That old man?"

"That old man," snorted Pete, "is Jack Hood, one of the best of 'em with a gun. But if it wasn't the fight that made you feel your oats, was it breaking Diablo?"

"No breaking to it. We just got acquainted."

"But what's happened? What's wakened you, Bull?"

"I dunno," said Bull and became thoughtful.

"Pete," he said, after a long time, "have you ever noticed a sort of a chill that gets inside you when the right sort of a girl smiles and—"

"The devil," murmured Pete Reeve; "it's the girl that's happened to you, eh? You forget her, Bull. I'm going to take you on the trail with me and keep you from thinking. It's a new trail for me, Bull. It's a trail where I'm going straight. I can't take you with me while I'm playing against the law. So I'm going to stay inside the law—with you."

"Maybe," and Bull Hunter sighed. "But no matter how far the trail leads, I'm thinking that some day I'll ride in a circle and come back to this place where we started out together."

He turned in the saddle.

The outline of the Dunbar house was fading into the night.

THE WHITE WOLF

MAX BRAND

"Brand is a topnotcher!"
—*New York Times*

Tucker Crosden breeds his dogs to be champions. Yet even by the frontiersman's brutal standards, the bull terrier called White Wolf is special. With teeth bared and hackles raised, White Wolf can brave any challenge the wilderness throws in his path. And Crosden has great plans for the dog until it gives in to the blood-hungry laws of nature. But Crosden never reckons that his prize animal will run at the head of a wolf pack one day—or that a trick of fate will throw them together in a desperate battle to the death.

_3870-6 $4.50 US/$5.50 CAN

Dorchester Publishing Co., Inc.
65 Commerce Road
Stamford, CT 06902

Please add $1.75 for shipping and handling for the first book and $.50 for each book thereafter. NY, NYC, PA and CT residents, please add appropriate sales tax. No cash, stamps, or C.O.D.s. All orders shipped within 6 weeks via postal service book rate. Canadian orders require $2.00 extra postage and must be paid in U.S. dollars through a U.S. banking facility.

Name_____

Address_____

City _____ State_____ Zip_____

I have enclosed $_____in payment for the checked book(s).

Payment <u>must</u> accompany all orders.☐ Please send a free catalog.

MAX BRAND

TROUBLE IN TIMBERLINE

"Brand is a topnotcher!"
—New York Times

Barney Dwyer is too big and too awkward to be much good around a ranch. But foreman Dan Peary has the perfect job for him. It seems Peary's son has joined up with a ruthless gang in the mountain town of Timberline, and Peary wants Barney to bring the no-account back, alive. Before long, Barney finds himself up to his powerful neck in trouble—both from gunslingers who defy the law and tin stars who are sworn to uphold it!

_3848-X $4.50 US/$5.50 CAN

RIP-ROARIN' ACTION AND ADVENTURE BY THE WORLD'S MOST CELEBRATED WESTERN WRITER!

Renowned throughout the Old West, Lucky Bill has the reputation of a natural battler. Yet he is no remorseless killer. He only outdraws any gunslinger crazy enough to pull a six-shooter first. Then Bill finds himself on the wrong side of the law, and plenty of greenhorns and gringos set their sights on collecting the price on his head. But Bill refuses to turn tail and run. He swears he'll clear his name and live a free man before he'll be hunted down and trapped like an animal.

_3937-0 $4.50 US/$5.50 CAN

RONICKY DOONE'S TREASURE

"Brand is a topnotcher!"
—New York Times

A horsebreaker, mischief-maker, and adventurer by instinct, Ronicky Doone dares every gunman in the West to outdraw him—and he always wins. But nothing prepares him for the likes of Jack Moon and his wild bunch. Hunting down a fortune in hidden loot, the desperadoes swear to string up or shoot down anyone who stands in their way. When Doone crosses their path, he needs a shootist's skill and a gambler's luck to survive, and if that isn't enough, his only reward will be a pine box.

_3748-3 $3.99 US/$4.99 CAN

TIMBAL GULCH TRAIL

"Brand is a topnotcher!"
—*New York Times*

Les Burchard owns the local gambling palace, half the town, and most of the surrounding territory, and Walt Devon's thousand-acre ranch will make him king of the land. The trouble is, Devon doesn't want to sell. In a ruthless bid to claim the spread, Burchard tries everything from poker to murder. But Walt Devon is a betting man by nature, even when the stakes are his life. The way Devon figures, the odds are stacked against him, so he can either die alone or take his enemy to the grave with him.

_3828-5 $4.50 US/$5.50 CAN